HANNAH'S HOLIDAY

Noelene Jenkinson

Chapter 1

Hannah sat up in bed with a jolt, her heart pounding. The dream again. The same screech of brakes and looking down on the accident scene in horror from above. Seeing it all unfold before her eyes as if in slow motion. The dreaded feeling of inability to do anything about it or warn them. Surreal because she hadn't been there or witnessed anything.

She closed her eyes and practised her usual deep breathing technique until her anxiety eased. She knew what had stirred up the turmoil again of course. The first anniversary of that fateful day. Her sisters had wanted to make something of it. Like a private family pilgrimage. Hannah didn't and refused to join them in their sombre graveside ceremony.

She couldn't face the cemetery and hadn't returned since all four girls had stood together in a huddle a year ago, stunned that both parents had been snatched from their lives so suddenly, and together.

Hannah thrust aside the doona, swung her

legs over the side of the bed and pushed her feet into slippers. This had to stop. The memories. The nightmares. She had tried, remained living in the family Cotswold home but discovered she was constantly badgered by her subconscious compounding her unreasonable guilt. A nagging whisper and the pain of remembrance urged her to escape.

So, with her three sisters' blessings, since she was the only one still living in the family home after their parents' deaths, she had boosted her confidence with a few stiff glasses of wine, spun a world globe, closed her eyes and poked.

Australia!

Could it have been any further away? Hannah had peered closer at where her finger landed. Victoria. Way down the bottom of Australia. A mere hop step and jump from Antarctica. She felt hugely disappointed it wasn't a warm and sunny Queensland beach and contemplated trying again but found she didn't care. What did it matter where she went?

'You're going where?' Chelsea demanded when she told her sisters.

Hannah knew it sounded ridiculous. 'You heard.'

'Crumbs, Han, what are you thinking?'

'That's the point, Chels, I don't plan to.'

After that, all Hannah had needed was a house swap in the area, available pretty much like, now.

Even as she trotted along Broadway high street to the travel office, made arrangements and stuffed her airline tickets into her oversized shoulder bag, she still questioned not just the necessity but the sanity of this radical move. Too crazy? Too far?

Well, she had loved *The Holiday* movie where Kate Winslet swapped her quaint cottage in Surrey for a swish LA mansion with Cameron Diaz. She hardly expected the romance. That was bottom of her list. Who would want a neurotic mess like her anyway?

Her particular swap was the Charles' family cottage in the Cotswolds for a renovated chapel in the small Australian country town of Tingara. Inland. Hours from anywhere like Melbourne or civilisation it seemed.

How mad was that?

She would give it a shot. If it didn't work she would pack up and head somewhere else for the remainder of her planned three months away. With her combined sick leave not taken for years and holidays way overdue, she could stay longer. She could go anywhere in the world she chose. Probably should have sooner. Like the day after her parents' joint funerals. But back then it would have felt like she was running away. At least she had persevered long enough to see if she could overcome her grief and stick it out.

But twelve months on, her emotions were still

raw, her life upside down as a result, so that she worked late, ate poorly. Took every opportunity to babysit her sister Heather's children so she didn't have to endure the deep aching loneliness of returning to the empty family home.

For the first time in her life she became highly aware of her single status and utter lack of a social life. She always joked that Heather and the kids made up for it but now it just plain hurt. She needed to make a change. She knew she was a valued member of the Oxford accountancy firm and had left her options open.

But, crumbs, at this point in her life, tens of thousands of feet above the earth flying east from England somewhere above Russia or Asia, heading for the smallest continent on the planet that floated between the Indian and Pacific oceans, she wasn't even sure she wanted to return to work or even England. What was back there? True, her three sisters, but they all lived their own lives. As she should, too. She knew options existed but she needed to know what they were before she could put them into place, right?

Gripped by yet another yawn, Hannah's mouth gaped and she blinked hard to stay awake. Jet lagged and knackered, she was beyond exhausted. It didn't help that her throat felt like sand paper every time she swallowed. She had blown and sneezed her way through a box of tissues and sucked on a whole packet of orange lozenges during the four hour drive up from Melbourne airport. This was nothing like England. It took so long to get anywhere in Australia. Which only emphasised its vast distances.

Now, gripping the wheel until her knuckles were white of her house swapper, Ginny's, luxurious and comfortable two-door BMW coupe, conveniently left at the airport, Hannah peered into the darkness, her headlights the only illumination between sparse street lamps as she crawled through the small country town of Tingara, searching for her destination.

Her heart pounded. Back home, driving still bothered her so she had taken to carpooling with other locals. Trying to overcome this ridiculous phobia about getting behind the wheel of a car, Hannah had crawled along the highway barely travelling at the speed limit, hugging the white line to the side of her lane, terrified, enduring the four draining hours to her destination.

'At the end of the main street, Ginny said. You can't miss it,' Hannah muttered wryly.

Great that they drove on the left hand side of the road over here, same as back home in England. The outspread branches of bare deciduous trees loomed at her as she passed. Fingers crossed this wild idea didn't bomb. She would be bored out of her brain if the town was dull. But then it couldn't be any less rural than her home village of Snowshill. And Ginny had assured her as a tourist town, Tingara hummed, especially on weekends, so she stayed hopeful.

Finally her bleary gaze latched onto the street sign she sought. Gum Tree Lane. Brilliant. Hannah heaved a grateful sigh and turned left.

'Only church in the street. Right hand side,' she muttered, repeating Ginny's instructions, her head turned, neck craned, frowning as she searched, barely able to see in the murky night.

'Ah. Home.'

She used the word lightly. For three months anyway while her fellow participant reaped the benefits of an English summer living in the Charles family's chocolate box cottage in England's postcard beautiful Cotswolds, Hannah had been plunged into the miserable depths of an approaching winter in a small Australian country town, half way across and down the bottom of the world.

In her fatigue, Hannah forgot to indicate as she turned into the driveway beside the church. It hardly mattered. Not like there was any other traffic about at this time of night and probably not much more during daytime as well, she predicted. In the headlights, the exterior glared so she guessed it was painted white which was enough really because she imagined the stained glass Gothic windows all around must be a glorious enough decorative feature on their own. She looked forward to appreciating them properly in daylight.

Oh, good. An exterior light automatically came on as she pulled up in the narrow gravelled driveway by a small porch. It was little more than a roof and timber frame sheltering the side door entrance and inset either side halfway up with stained glass panels.

She dipped her head and glanced out the front windscreen. What she could see of it was small and cute and certainly looked like a church.

She turned off the ignition, stretched and shivered as she unscrambled her weary body from inside the warm car to be hit by a blast of nippy night air. She hugged her coat more closely around her and trotted under the porch. In the dark, Hannah couldn't see Ginny's garden but could smell the scent of something vaguely minty wafting into her tired dull senses.

The real estate agent, Anne Perry, was supposed to leave a key under the doormat. Not very original but it was there when she lifted it up, glinting in the half light. Mere photographs of this little church had enticed her halfway around the world. At the moment she just felt rubbish and wanted to crawl into bed. Hopefully it was as comfortable inside as it looked from the outside. It certainly appeared promising and was definitely unique. In a mad desperate moment, its architecture alone had convinced her to up stakes from her stressful life and make this crazy journey.

Apart from the internet photos of a church conversion proving enticing, the similarities between her swapper, Ginny's, life and her own had been eerie. Workaholics. No social life. Both professional women with careers instead of family.

At least she'd been able to sleep in her comfortable business class seat and bed she had splurged on for the tedious lengthy flight. Twenty four hours. Who did that?

Taking extended leave was not a problem. Hannah was almost ashamed she hadn't taken a single vacation for over four years. But she was forced to admit that her life *was* starting to affect her health.

Often feeling miserable and harried, without fail she had still endured the daily commute and struggled into work every day. Few of her friendships survived the burdensome life she led. And to her embarrassment, only a handful of fellow co-workers bothered to say goodbye when she left. A straggly half-hearted group gathered to say farewell, making her realise how little she had really known them.

Hannah's numb and blue fingers fumbled with the key to unlock the huge timber Gothic arched front door to enter a compact vestibule, originally the church entrance. With the help of the pale outside light from the open door, she patted the wall until she found the power switch. With her temporary home now revealed in flooding light, Hannah's gaze swept the scene. Gobsmacked, her jaw dropped and she smiled. Strings of tension loosened in her body and she relaxed. Gosh, it was gorgeous. The bee's knees for sure and ticked every box of her expectation. Time would tell if Tingara measured up, too.

She walked straight into a huge open space with a lofty ceiling and exposed timber beams. To her right at the slightly raised altar end, a country style timber and white kitchen had been installed. She imagined on sunny days it would be flooded with light from the stained glass and diamond paned Gothic windows above.

Directly in front of her was a small table setting with timber backed pews for seating. Further to her left was an electric or gas log fireplace set into the wall surrounded by plush deep sofas. Oh, Heaven, she sighed deeply with weary pleasure. Then realised the pun. Even in her present state of illness and exhaustion she managed to raise a grin.

But at the far end of the church - well, it was a house now, wasn't it? - the masterpiece of the entire renovation in Hannah's thinking was the addition of a short curved timber staircase up to a mezzanine bedroom level. She curbed a squeal of delight. She would be sleeping up there?

Her excitement carried her at a jog back out to the car to wheel in her two suitcases. One by one, she hauled them up the thankfully short flight of stairs. She visited the en suite loo that was an auto sensing flush thing, almost screamed at the sight of a gleaming white spa bath, then shed her crumpled clothes to litter the floor - something she would never dream of doing at home - and changed into pyjamas. Normally a neat and control freak, at this ghastly hour of the morning Hannah skipped cleaning her teeth but merely snapped off the lights and collapsed into the generous feather-soft bed, dragging the doona around her to snuggle beneath.

Her last happy thought was of the obvious and sheer indulgent luxury of Ginny's little renovated haven. She should have guessed that a head-hunted CEO would own nothing less. Or so she said. This house swap gig might turn out all right after all. Tomorrow would tell, she sighed, as she sank quick sticks into exhausted sleep.

Awareness returned to Hannah with the rude insistent buzzing of her mobile vibrating on the bedside table, pulling her from the depths of, for once, a contented if jetlag-induced sleep.

She groped for her phone and frowned in a drowsy squint against its bright light.

Before she could speak a cheery demanding voice said, 'Hannah, honey, it's Ginny.'

What was she doing phoning from England? At this Godforsaken hour? Hannah groaned, praying nothing was wrong.

Miserable and grumpy, she blurted out, 'Hi. It's one a.m. here. What do you want?'

'I know, honey. I thought I'd catch you before you went to bed.'

'Too late,' Hannah muttered.

Ginny either didn't hear or didn't care because she powered on. 'Just a few rules for you about St. Anne's. Don't ever let that damned stray cat inside. He'll destroy my leather sofas.'

Hannah frowned. She hadn't seen any cat when she arrived.

'Turn the mattress on my bed every other week.'

This was a king sized bed. Did she know how big and heavy it must be?

'And don't sleep on the same side. Alternate. Not that I often slept alone.' She gave a throaty laugh. 'And the whole chapel needs to be thoroughly cleaned every week.'

'You don't have a cleaner?' Hannah managed to squeak, sensing this sojourn was not going to be a holiday, even though she and housework were best friends.

'Oh, I gave her time off while you're there.'

'How considerate,' Hannah said wryly. She had scrubbed and vacuumed their own cottage before leaving and arranged for a local lady to come in twice weekly to check all remained in order.

'I do pride myself on looking after my

employees. Now, I usually eat out or at Will's. There are lots of quaint places to eat in town but if you *do* decide to cook or, God forbid, bring in takeaway food, please run the kitchen exhaust fan for at least an hour afterwards to dispel any odours.

Hannah clenched her teeth, barely able to keep her eyes open and astonished at this list of orders. 'Of course.' And planning to ignore them.

'Now, I didn't have time before I left but I'll whip off an email to you with all the rules and note down a few other points to help you out.'

Hannah grew weary just listening to this dynamo spouting instructions from the other side of the world. She had gradually slumped from sitting upright on the bed since being jolted awake by this thoughtless call, fell back to reclining and was now sliding under the covers again.

'I hope you enjoy your new job.' What else could she say? She just wanted this livewire to stop talking and hang up so she could get back to sleep. Ginny had sounded so much friendlier when they first made contact and agreed to swap.

'Oh, it's going to be wonderful. PR for the rich and famous is just fabulous, honey. A career tailor made for me.'

'Good.' Hannah wondered what her work entailed but clearly Ginny read her mind because she presumed an explanation was expected.

'I squash stories, honey. Liaise with wealthy and famous clients, opposition lawyers, that kind of thing. Arrange *settlements*,' she crooned, lowering her voice.

Hannah imagined her winking, expecting her listener to understand what she meant. She hadn't a clue.

'Help clients sell juicy stories,' Ginny rolled on. 'A hint here and there, a teaser of gossip. All feeds the media who feed careers. It takes skill and strategy controlling them I can tell you. The tiniest snippet can raise an individual's profile. They need to be *handled*,' she emphasised, 'carefully and, sometimes, discreetly.' Then before Hannah could ask how Ginny was settling into the cottage, she ended the call with a blunt, 'I'll be in touch.'

No apology for waking Hannah in the middle of the night and leaving her with the unanswered question of who on earth was Will? On that thought she flicked her phone to silent and instantly dropped off to sleep again.

'You must do something, William. Ginny asked you to keep an eye on the English girl and no one's seen her for days.'

Will Bennett smiled indulgently at his neighbour, Alma Powell, and fellow resident of Gum Tree Lane. 'Don't want to intrude on the poor woman's privacy when she's hardly landed.' Remembering with no great fondness those long international flights during his backpacking years.

'Oh, you're slack at the best of times,' she scoffed. 'Just go check on her and make sure she's all right.'

'Why don't you go? She mightn't appreciate a foreign Aussie bloke chatting her up.'

'Not my place. Ginny told *you*.'

Will would guarantee the girl, Hannah someone apparently, only two days out from travelling halfway around the world was probably jet lagged, still only half awake and operating on auto pilot. He had already walked past the church and checked. Ginny's sexy little black sports number was parked in the driveway, smoked billowed in drifts from the chimney during the day and the lights came on at night. Whoever was in St. Anne's was alive and probably appreciating their privacy.

'She'll surface eventually.'

'But what's she doing for food? I haven't seen her go to the shops.'

'I'm sure she's surviving.'

'William, you're too casual by far. If you don't investigate that girl today, I won't give you that ginger cake recipe you love.'

'Yes you will. I'll charm it out of you,' he grinned.

Alma was mostly hot air but her heart was

pure gold. He knew her motive in wanting to scope out the new arrival. Gossip. It was a miracle her short legs hadn't already carried her across the Lane to introduce herself to the visitor. The restraint was epic and probably killing her. He decided to relent. He had planned on heading three doors down sometime today anyway.

'As you wish.'

Alma wagged a finger at him. 'Just make sure the poor thing's okay.'

'Want me to report back?' he teased.

'Oh, go on with you. Of course I do. Every little detail.'

A short time later, Will huddled in the shelter of St. Anne's porch and rapped on the door. It was an impressive beast of a thing and he almost broke the skin on his knuckles with the effort. At first he heard no sound or movement from inside. He checked the watch he rarely wore. It had gone ten so he thumped again with his fist, louder. Eventually, coughing and shuffling followed before the huge door slowly creaked open and a deathly pale but rather gorgeous sweet face peered outside.

Long tangled blonde hair fell in a soft and messy tumble about her face and shoulders and halfway down her back. One errant tendril clung to one of her arms that hugged a soft blue printed dressing gown tightly about her. It screamed designer label. Liberty maybe? Similar to the style his sister Courtney chose, too.

His first thought was *What an angel. English roses do exist then.* There was limited opportunity in Tingara to meet females. Not just because of the small population but those nudging forty were usually already taken. He didn't believe he did this woman an injustice by his thoughts because he gauged her to be a similar age to his own. Nothing less than a very pleasant surprise.

'Yes?' she squinted, sounding grumpy.

'Sorry if I disturbed you-'

'You didn't. I was awake. What do you want?' she scowled at him and the pot of soup he carried in a handled earthenware container.

'Just called to say hello and make sure you're okay.'

She tucked long strands of hair behind her ears. 'Clearly I'm alive,' she said crisply, 'and I'm perfectly happy to be left alone.'

'Okay, Princess.'

The woman visibly bristled with offence. 'Excuse me?'

He grinned. 'You have quite the posh English accent there.'

Clearly startled by his comment, she snapped, 'Never thought of myself as a ponce. I have a virus. I may be contagious,' she warned, moving to close the door.

'Brought you a pot of vegetable and pasta soup. My version of minestrone. Substantial stuff. Should do for a couple meals. Welcome to the neighbourhood.' He thrust the container toward her, forcing her to open the door wider to accept. In surprise, he noticed. 'Name's Will.' When she didn't return the introduction, he added, 'I'll leave you to it then. I live further down the Lane.' He waved vaguely toward the street.

Once his gift was safely transferred into her care, he turned with a wave, jammed his hands into his pockets and sauntered back down the driveway.

Chapter 2

So, *that* was Will. Hannah stared after him. Apparently Ginny spent a lot of time in his company. At least, eating his food, judging by the comments made during the inconsiderate woman's nocturnal phone call.

As he strolled away, Hannah was left with the impression of a quiet chap, misguided sense of humour - at her expense - and a wicked arse. He was all a bit mysterious and annoyingly charismatic. Your typical hippy bad boy. He wasn't young but then neither was she. She would guess he'd been around the block a few times. No crime in that except it had given him a wary edge, betrayed by that drilling gaze. For all his bohemian simplicity and air of gentleness, Hannah considered him worldly.

She might still have a foggy brain but was aware enough to appreciate a man who was different and intriguing. His long sandy hair was pulled back and caught in a loose pony tail, its straggly ends floating about his face.

Yet his external image conflicted with his

polite manner. The baggy pants, long loose jumper and paisley scarf clashed with a voice that suggested at the least a good education, possibly private. Upper class even. Will whoever-he-was looked as far removed from a stereotype as it was possible to be.

As Hannah was about to kick the heavy porch door shut with her foot, the friendly neighbourhood cat Ginny mentioned shot inside.

'Morning Fluffy.' The name was a feeble no brainer. It was the furriest feline Hannah had ever seen. She personally disliked the exotic hairless designer varieties, so her heart had melted at first sight and willingly welcomed her into the church, Ginny's warning demand ringing in her ears.

With Fluffy mewing about her ankles, Hannah set the soup pot on the kitchen counter. It was still hot and smelled delicious. Had he made it himself or brought it on behalf of another cook? A female perhaps? A chap like that surely wouldn't live alone.

She had been jolted by his sudden appearance and friendly gesture, her first sight of another human being since arrival. Her own fault. She had felt so miserable, a mixture of her recurring grief, poor health and jet lag.

Crumbs. What must the chap have thought of her scruffy appearance? She shouldn't feel bothered. He was a stranger and likely to stay that way in the light of her recent unsociable ways back home. But then she simply hadn't made the time. Now she had bags of it.

Hannah showered and dressed before making tea and toast for breakfast, the soup pot sitting like a nagging magnetic temptation on the counter. Did people eat soup for breakfast? Since sparking up a bit in the past twenty four hours, her appetite had also returned. While it was still hot, why not try a sample?

She dipped in a soup spoon and her taste buds exploded into life. This nosh was *so good* and it was lovely to eat home cooking again. So far, between long nights of sleep and daytime naps, she had survived on a couple of frozen meals Ginny had left in the freezer which she zapped in the microwave, plus a bowl full of cereal with a splash of long life milk she found in Ginny's virtually empty pantry.

She scratched around for a ladle in the utensil drawer and scooped out enough of the liquid meal to fill a bowl. She ate up every drop, snuggled on a sofa in front of the ambient electric fake log fire with Fluffy draped across her feet, feeling properly satisfied for the first time since arriving. She poured the remaining soup into a lidded container, stowed it in the refrigerator and washed the pot.

It only took an hour to Hoover, clean and tidy the house after which she stood in the middle of downstairs wondering what to do next. She could rug up and take a walk, explore the town. She could return the soup pot to the chap Will. If she knew where he lived. Crumbs. At this rate, with no purpose in her life, she would go mad by the end of her first week. What on earth would she do with the other eleven?

She hadn't needed to think of alternatives back home in recent years because her life revolved around work, caring for her aging parents since moving back into the family home and mostly being there for her two youngest sisters, as well as Heather and her boys.

Her winter holiday yawned ahead with scary uncertainty and potential boredom. Well, this was a vacation, right? She would take herself off sightseeing. Must be an information office in town if the area was the tourist mecca Ginny claimed. Especially weekends, she'd said. What was today? Saturday. Tingara was probably humming. She *should* get out amongst it but found the idea daunting. She'd not know a soul. It was taking that first daunting step with any measure of confidence. Odd, because in her career she worked with people all day.

It was all right for Ginny. Judging by their couple of video calls, she was a big marketing person who lapped up the social life so she wouldn't have time to feel lost. Hannah suspected she wouldn't spend much time in the village or cottage back home anyway.

For the first time, Hannah questioned if she

had made the wrong choice and would regret this snap house swap decision. No. Fluffy stretched out in front of the heater, eyes half closed in bliss. She would stay at home for one more day. Read, doze and eat more soup. All the while muttering to herself *coward.*

Later, her sense of duty kicked in and nagged her subconscious. Because the time was right and connected back home - it would be early morning in England - Hannah made the regretful decision to text and email her sisters. It had been days since she'd checked her phone messages and logged on. Bleary with illness and misery, the world had been temporarily forgotten.

With the iPad in her lap, she opened her mail and clicked through. Ginny's email sat like a glaring teacher's lecture at the top. She scrolled down. It was pages long! Hannah pressed Delete and moved on to the rest.

She closed her eyes and sighed, realising how truly peaceful her recent days had been. Even halfway across the world, her siblings still sought her advice - usually ignored - and readily shared their petty dramas. Often involving each other.

Since their parents' deaths and being the eldest, although all four were adults now, Hannah had assumed responsibility. Heavy guilt and obligation kept her firmly anchored in her sisters' lives.

Driven by a growing need to be left alone wherever she was in the world, Hannah was tempted to turn off all her electronic devices and ignore everything. At least digitally she could disappear.

What a fanciful thought. Dare she? Abandon the cries in front of her reading like a wailing litany?

Why did you go away? Why did you have to go so far? Heather.

I need you. Chelsea.

I can't decide. What should I do about-? Victoria.

Like she could do anything about any of it from over here. Anyway with her lack of life's experience, what qualifications did she have to dispense advice? Tucked away in the rural depths of England only having had one mad romantic and totally unwise fling with David for six months three years ago.

So she fielded questions and gave brief answers, feeling bad to still claim ill health when she was slowly feeling better every day, and promising to contact them again soon. Begging their patience to give her time to recover. Deliberately pulling back. An oddly strange and uplifting state of affairs. Although she would miss babysitting Heather's boys, her lively pre-schooler nephews, Andrew and James.

Hopefully the coming months would allow her time to reflect on her life and where she wanted to go from here. More than dwelling on the loss of both her parents at once and feeling responsible.

She knew if she was to achieve the purpose of this holiday, she must learn to ease away from being so available to her sisters. Brainstorm how her life should change when she returned. How to not only reclaim a life of her own again but balance work and time to herself. Try to establish a social life. Not that she ever really had one. Even while at university, Hannah had knowingly sacrificed deep or lasting relationships to work multiple part time jobs to pay for her education.

So, the rest of her life started tomorrow.

Many nights when she minded Andy and James, smelt them fresh from the bath and read them stories all snuggled together, the seeds of yearning were sown in Hannah for children of her own. But to accomplish that she needed to work less, get herself out onto the social dating scene and find a chap. It wasn't a new thought but one that festered in the back of her mind in recent years. Ever since her hot and desperate but short lived affair with David ended badly when she grew broody and clingy, making her vulnerable. And hurt when, in the end, David dumped her and ran.

Maybe she could make more of an effort to forge a new relationship when she returned home.

Meanwhile, on holiday here in Tingara,

Australia, she must somehow learn to slow down and relax again. Enjoy her own company. Embrace her freedom.

That evening over yet another big serving of hot nourishing soup and a mug of tea, Hannah experienced the first stirrings of confusion, having no clue yet how best to go about effecting the change she knew she needed. Now that she had caught up on deep jet lagged sleep, exaggerated dreams haunted her nights again, making her grateful for the dawn.

Next morning, feeling better after lingering in the deep bath tub before dressing for warmth in jeans, a hugging tee shirt and long woolly tunic sweater, Hannah trotted downstairs for breakfast, washed the dishes and tidied up before braving a search to find her welcoming neighbour Will. Hopefully at least one other person would appear on the street to ask directions.

Out of habit, Hannah stuffed her mobile phone into her pocket and, for the first time in days with the soup pot under one arm, she stepped outdoors into the sharp and frosty winter morning air. She had eyed the cottage garden through the church windows of course but not really taken it all in. This morning however her perception was so clear it was like a light bulb being switched on and all about her was viewed with fresh technicolour eyes.

Hannah hesitated on the footpath. Left or

right? Will said he lived further down the Lane so she turned away from the direction of the main street where she had driven in a few nights ago and headed along the footpath and grassy verges between houses and road. Tall trees lined the Lane, presumably gums after its name, parading in either direction like an avenue. The homes were mostly single level brick or timber bungalows, unlike England's storied stone cottages, and not hugging the street as was familiar to Hannah but set back from it on large blocks surrounded by lawns and gardens with a driveway and garage for cars.

As she walked, a boy approached on a bicycle. 'Excuse me. Do you know where Will lives?' The child shook his head and rode on.

Two doors down across the street, a lady appeared at her mailbox out on the front picket fence. Not a slot in the front door like most houses in England. Hannah approached and repeated her question.

The elderly woman's interest was immediate and bright. 'Oh you must be Ginny's lodger for the winter. Can tell by your English accent of course. Come for a holiday then?'

'Yes.' Easier to avoid explanations.

'Well you've certainly come to the right place. Tingara's nice and quiet. You'll be able to have a lovely rest here."

Just hope I won't be bored. 'I'm looking for Will's place?'

'Of course you are.' She nodded her grey wavy head in the direction Hannah had been heading. 'Keep going. Big mud brick house on your side of the Lane further down. Different from all the others. Bit like Will, really.' She grinned and glanced at the pot in Hannah's arms. 'Did you enjoy the soup?'

'Very much.'

'Alma,' she introduced herself. 'Need anything, just ask. We won't bite.'

'Hannah. Nice to meet you. Cheers, then.'

'Don't bother with Will's front door,' Alma called after her. 'Just go round the back. It's still early so he might not be up yet.'

Hannah felt the woman's eyes on her as she walked away. Not surprising, she supposed, being a stranger to a small town and foreign at that. She well knew from village life in England how gossip soon made its rounds. She didn't mind so long as everyone left her in peace. After the last few days on her own with no one to please but herself, even if she did feel rubbish, it was a strangely indulgent feeling to not be at others' beck and call for a change. She'd find Will, drop off his pot and get back to her peaceful freedom.

Alma was right. The mud brick house did rather announce itself to anyone on the Lane who passed. Painted a drab neutral colour, the bungalow blended into its tranquil setting and nestled comfortably within its bush garden.

Although distinctly bohemian like its owner, because of its very difference it bore an unexpectedly homely appeal.

Despite Alma's advice, an intrigued Hannah crunched her way up the meandering gravel path to the front door, feeling it an intrusion to wander around the back onto a stranger's private property. She pressed the bell set into the wall beside the gloriously coloured stained glass front door. She wondered that any human was strong enough to open such a monstrous medieval looking thing. She admired the design while she waited for a response. After a while with no sounds answering her summons, she pressed the bell again. Still she waited.

With a sigh and feeling snoopy, there was nothing for it but to heed Alma's suggestion. Cautiously, she found her way along yet another overgrown winding side path to seek out another entrance. When it opened out onto a brick paved courtyard, she halted for a moment in awe. The rear garden was stunning. Magical. Beautifully landscaped in the most carefree way with a pond, an orchard further back, raised winter vegetable garden beds abundant with produce, all now bathed in the first streams of wan early morning sun forcing their way through the dispersing foggy cloud.

When she turned back to the house and its wall of windows, Hannah caught her breath at the sight of Will standing before an easel, painting, in bare feet. Wasn't he cold? In the moments before he noticed her, she tried not to stare at the rather scruffy vision splendid, his long hair tied back again and catching the early light. He frowned in concentration, paused in his work and bent to stroke a fluffy black, ginger and white cat entwining itself between his legs.

She shivered in the biting air redolent with the smell of chimney smoke from wood fires and that minty aroma again she had first noticed on the night of her arrival. She should have worn gloves. Her fingers were blue with cold and beginning to feel numb.

As she stared, Will casually glanced up, showing no sign of surprise, as though she always appeared unannounced at his back door, and grinned. Feeling awkward and guilty, she gave a stupid wave through the French door and waited as he wiped his brush on a rag and sauntered to open it.

'I pressed your front bell but there was no answer,' she explained.

'Oh, it doesn't work,' he said easily as though she should know.

Taken aback by his indifference, she said, 'You should get it fixed.'

'No need. Everyone swings round the back.' He seemed amused by her discomfort.

She had been so abrupt with him yesterday, she was apprehensive about her reception today. Apart from his tendency to tease, he was being really *nice*.

'Alma said you might not be up yet.' She cringed the moment she said it. Sounded like criticism.

'Ah. That's because I usually paint at night when everyone else is asleep. Couldn't settle to it though last night.' His warm brown eyes searched her white face. 'But I was gripped by inspiration about four this morning. Come in.'

'Oh, I don't mean to stay.'

'You don't?' He appeared entertained by her strain.

Hannah thrust the pot toward him. 'The soup was lovely, thank you.'

'Lovely,' he repeated barely above a murmur. And grinned again. 'English accents are so … charming.'

'Especially a *posh* one?' she said wryly.

His eyebrows flickered in appreciation of her sense of humour but he didn't comment. Only moved closer and relieved her of the dish. Their hands brushed together in the exchange. Hannah quickly pulled back and defensively shoved her frozen hands into her sleeves against the cold.

'At least come inside for a moment and get warm again before you have to trot back to St. Anne's.'

Hannah's instinct was to escape but his invitation was quietly spoken and genuine, and the rush of warm air from inside proved too enticing to resist. Besides, she had nothing better to do and was nosy enough to want to see inside his house. She stepped across the threshold and Will quickly closed the door against the chill while the cat proceeded to investigate her ankles.

'Her name's Callie because of her calico tricolour,' he explained.

'She's gorgeous.'

'And spoilt, for want of another female in the house.'

That little gem of information was a surprise. Honestly? A chap at his age oozing all that charm and appeal without a steady partner? To be honest, he bordered on mildly sexy, inclined to chat up with veiled remarks and subtle comments making the other person aware and, in her case, self-conscious as well. He appealed in a shabby way. The kind of chap a woman might be tempted to smarten up. Maybe Will had a lover but she didn't live under his roof. For some reason, the idea was vaguely disappointing.

Without appearing too obvious, she darted a side glance toward his partly completed watercolour, perfectly placed in this casual light-filled space. It was a realistic Australian bush landscape and reminded Hannah of any number of quality English artists. This work showed equally considerable talent.

He caught her observation and she blushed.

'Sorry. Didn't mean to-'

He shrugged. 'I'm compiling my first solo exhibition for a small boutique city gallery. I hate deadlines and pressure but they've seen my work and want to promote me,' he said with easy honesty and a quick grin.

Such a prestigious accolade wasn't just offered to any old artist, Hannah was sure. Even with this painting a work-in-progress, it was clear he had a definite gift. 'How exciting for you.'

'We'll see how it goes.' He scratched his head and for the first time looked almost awkward in her presence. 'I haven't eaten breakfast yet. I don't do coffee but I can offer you tea while I boil up some porridge.'

Hannah discovered herself loath to refuse. She *had* planned to scuttle away as soon as possible but a man who drank tea? Too endearing. Most of the men she knew either drank pints in the pub or slurped down mugs of coffee at their desks while they worked.

So she found herself saying, 'That would be lovely.'

This unassuming confident person was an enigma. Hannah usually encountered brash ladder-climbing men in suits. Will's quiet uncomplicated presence was a refreshing change but, while his garden was impressive, indoors was an untidy jumble. Fair enough that his paints and brushes were everywhere in chaotic colour about his easel and working canvas but as she followed him from the sunroom studio through to a vast and well equipped rustic kitchen, chaos reigned.

An old black cast iron wood burning stove pumped out serious warmth and a huge scrubbed timber table dominated the centre but daily living *stuff* littered half its surface. Pens and papers, a stack of books, while above hung an array of pots and bunches of dried herbs. The sink opposite overflowed with dirty dishes.

She couldn't bear living like this. It all looked clean enough underneath, the slate floor gleamed but after the pristine order of St. Anne's, Hannah realised that not everyone was a neat freak. People like this Will seemed unaffected by the disorder around them. For Hannah, everything had its place.

From a pottery canister, he spooned oats, adding milk and water with a pinch of salt and brown sugar into a small saucepan and set it to one side of the stove top to cook. Then he scooped tea leaves into a dark stoneware teapot with an arched cane handle and poured over hot water from a simmering cast iron kettle. While it steeped, Hannah unwound, comfortable enough in his presence, unthreatened, feeling no particular need for conversation, content to silently soak up the unconventional surroundings, rife with Will's distinctive personality, the mark of a creative soul.

He stirred the porridge then produced a pottery mug from a glass fronted overhead cupboard and poured her tea.

'Where do you live in England?' He pushed the mug toward her.

'Thank you.' She cupped her hands around it for warmth. 'The Cotswolds.'

His eyebrows flickered. 'Ah. An area of outstanding natural beauty and a photographer's paradise. Do you work in the county?'

She shook her head. 'I commute to Oxford.'

'You won't need any transport in Tingara. It's only a fifteen minute walk anywhere. What do you do in Oxford?'

'I'm an accountant.'

He turned back from stirring his porridge again. 'You don't look like one.'

'What should an accountant look like?'

He shrugged. 'Probably your stereotype man in a suit. Certainly not a gorgeous woman.'

Hannah grew confused by the compliment.

After a brief clinical gaze, Will said, 'You're very pale. With your notorious English climate and working indoors, you should take Vitamin D.'

'Should I?' So observant. Judging by his clothes, home and garden, he was probably into all that natural herbal stuff.

'So, how did you choose where to go for your holiday?'

Warming and relaxed, Hannah sighed and said cautiously, 'I was over everything. Hadn't taken a holiday for years. Just worked and cared for our ageing parents.' No need to mention the lack of any social life. 'So I just closed my eyes and stuck my finger on the laptop screen on Google maps to choose a property from the holiday house swap website. When I looked, it was St. Anne's. I almost tried again when I saw it was so far away. But I've never travelled and I thought, well, why not?'

'Maddest thing you've ever done?'

'Absolutely.'

He paused, his voice low. 'Any one at home pining your absence?'

Hannah thought of her sisters but he meant a man. Cheeky lad. She shook her head.

'Regrets?' he prompted.

She levelled his steady gaze. 'Not yet. Early days though.'

Steady, Hannah. You live in England and you're only here for three months. But a saucy voice in her head taunted *You're not a child. You've had a fling. You know what it's all about.*

Chapter 3

'How are you settling into St Anne's then?' Will eased the conversation onto less dangerous ground.

'It's beautifully done and furnished inside. High spec.'

'Ginny insisted. I helped her redesign and convert it.'

'It's just lovely,' Hannah enthused. 'You had some great ideas.'

'It's my job. I'm an architect.'

'Really?'

'I know. Don't look like one, do I?' he drawled.

Touché, Hannah thought and laughed, noting the irony that apparently neither of them were what they seemed. Probably best to bury her prejudice right now. Will watched her with deep fascination. She had become toasty warm since being indoors again but now she heated even further with embarrassment as he stared.

'Ginny expects nothing less than the best,' he added, his gaze never leaving her face.

'I did gain that impression. I hope she's not disappointed in our cottage back home.'

Will chuckled. 'Trust me, if she was, you'd have heard about it by now.'

Hannah had already received a blast but on other matters. She sipped her tea. 'Have you always lived in Tingara then?'

Will shook his head. 'Grew up here but my family moved to Melbourne. My parents were determined their children receive a private school education.'

Hannah detected a hint of bitterness creep into his usually pleasant tone. But the information explained the influence behind his cultured voice.

'You seem meant for country life,' she observed, glancing about. 'How did you end up back here in Tingara?'

'Long story.' He turned away to retrieve the saucepan, stir the contents and spoon the porridge into a large bowl.

'Sorry.' Hannah said softly, grasping Will's reluctance to talk. 'Didn't mean to intrude.'

'You're not. You don't know me.' He hesitated, his gaze softening as he pulled out a stool opposite and began eating his breakfast. 'It took years but I finally realised Tingara is where I belong.'

'Are your parents still alive?' He nodded. 'You're lucky. Mine are both dead.' Hannah surprised herself by the admission. She usually found it almost impossible to speak of them. Memories and guilt still cut deep so she swiftly changed focus. 'I expect you see your folks often?'

'Heavens, no. Only when I must. They're professionals with crazy lives and long hours. We've never been close. They have little time to spare for their children.'

Stunned into silence for a moment by the blunt revelation, Hannah heard the tension in his voice resurface. Here she was with no parents, heavy with regret over their deaths and wishing them back. Will still had his parents, apparently didn't get on and sounded estranged. She pitied rather than envied him and wondered if he ever wished it otherwise.

Hoping she wasn't treading on another touchy subject, Hannah asked, 'So you have brothers and sisters?'

Here, Will livened up and Hannah's shoulders sagged with relief as she finished her tea.

Will paused over his breakfast. 'One of each as it happens. My sister Courtney is married with a two year old daughter, Charlotte, and our brother Lewis is the youngest and gay.' Will glowed when he spoke of them. Clearly his siblings were closer and more positive lights in his life.

'Are they in Melbourne?'

He nodded and resumed eating.

'Catch up often?'

'Texts and phone calls mostly,' he said between the last mouthful and scraping his bowl.

'You're in touch though. That's nice.'

He dumped his empty bowl into the sink with a clatter and poured himself a mug of tea from the pot. A reflective silence settled between them as each processed what they had learnt from the stranger sitting opposite.

Will leaned forward and rested his arms on the counter. She caught her breath at his too-soft gaze. 'So, do *you* have siblings?'

'Three sisters,' she said readily. Apart from reading their emails yesterday, Hannah realised how little she had thought of them since leaving England where they usually dominated her life. 'We're close. Probably too close really,' she admitted. 'After less than a week away I'm beginning to wonder if I haven't been too involved with them all.'

'Why do you say that?'

Hannah shrugged. 'I guess they rely on me.'

'Why?'

Because she let them take advantage and felt powerless to stop. 'Perhaps because I'm the oldest.'

'Are they married or single?'

'Heather's married with two boys. Pre-schoolers. She's in Oxford about forty miles away. An hour by car. The other two live in

London. Victoria works in hospitality. Floats around. Casual and part time mostly. Better pay rates. Chelsea loves fashion and works in a boutique. They both have a raging social life. Get invited to a *lot* of parties. They're both gorgeous,' she said, unable to conceal her envy with a sigh.

'You looked in a mirror lately?' Will asked softly. 'Don't underplay yourself.'

Hannah felt herself furiously blush. Men didn't usually figure in her life let alone chat her up. Will might be a quiet one but she'd have to watch him. Blondes like herself tended to be stereotyped as easy and dumb. Targets for chatting up but Will knew she had a brain so she trusted he thought more highly of her than that.

'I live in our family home. We haven't sold it yet.' Slightly depressing thought. She brightened. 'Just as well, else I wouldn't have been able to do this house swap.'

'So, you're an accountant, you have a bunch of sisters. What do you like to do?'

'Not cook, that's for sure,' she smiled through her sadness. 'To be honest, I rarely have the time or interest. Whatever's quick and easy when I'm tired really. Sometimes we all go to the Arms. Our local pub. My mother was the best cook. Roasts, pies, stews. And loads of baking.' A lump caught in Hannah's throat at the nostalgic recollection and she swallowed to bury it. Somehow she recovered and moved on. 'I'd like your soup recipe if you'll share it.'

'Don't have one really. Just make it up as I go along with whatever's in season and to hand. But just your basic stock. Chuck in a fistful of fresh herbs, any vegetables you have in the fridge. Maybe add a can of lentils. Boil pasta, done. Not rocket science,' he said humbly.

Hannah smiled at his slapdash method and silently admired his obvious culinary skills. Will would never starve or expect a woman to be in the kitchen. He was competent enough there himself. By comparison, she was never one to wing it. She needed a recipe.

'Well,' she slid off her stool, 'I might go shopping and give it a try. Thanks for the tea. I've taken up your time.' She gestured back toward his sunroom painting area.

'No you haven't. I invited you in, remember? It's been a pleasure getting to know you Hannah since we'll be neighbours for a few months.' He indicated for her to follow. 'Come out to the garden and I'll give you some fresh veggies and herbs to toss in your soup.'

At the French doors, he slid his bare feet into a pair of well-worn plastic Crocs. He held the door open for her as they emerged, making Hannah realise how cosy it had been inside as she caught her breath against the bleak chill. Will cut a small head of winter broccoli and cauliflower, bunches of herbs, pulled some carrots and a few huge leaves of silver beet, all of which he shook free of dirt and dew drops before thrusting them into her arms.

His generosity and the physical contact as their hands and arms touched in the shuffling transfer and acceptance of the load made her grow warm despite the nippy morning.

'Thank you.'

'I've plenty to spare. I usually supply neighbours and friends with the excess. Take your time when you go shopping. Do a walking tour of the town,' Will suggested. 'There's an historic bakery, the rotunda in the park and The Stables. Big old red brick building that's been converted into a craft market. Huge tourist draw card. My friend, Emma Hamilton, is a jeweller and works from there. Tell her I sent you.' He grinned.

'I will. Cheers,' she said as she staggered away under her armload of freshly picked produce. The fragrant smells drifting up from the herbs was wonderful.

Back at St. Anne's, Hannah stowed Will's bounty in the refrigerator, made herself a list of supplies and headed up the slight rise toward the top of Gum Tree Lane. Fellow shoppers acknowledged her with a smile or comment about the cold morning but the locals wouldn't yet know she was Ginny's English lodger unless she opened her mouth to speak.

In the process of her rambles, Hannah took her time and window shopped, unaccustomed to not feeling that sense of urgency all the time, that she must rush. Crumbs, back home she was always in a hurry, always checking her watch or the time on her mobile. She enjoyed her unhurried random browsing, discovering it a forgotten simple pleasure. There were all manner of wonderful unique shops supplying every tourist need and whim. A dedicated honey shop, a provender selling all local chutneys, jams, fine goods, cheeses and smoked meats, and tea rooms where she lingered over good coffee.

She was fascinated by the curved verandas over the front of every shop, the lacy wrought iron trims at the tops of corner posts. Tingara's old world atmosphere tended to ease you back into its slower small town pace. Other smartly dressed pedestrians in the high street must surely be tourists since they toted shopping bags and stepped in and out of gleaming luxury cars. Definitely urbanites.

When the biting air turned her nose and ears numb, and her fingertips blue, Hannah escaped into warm stores. Foolish of her not to toss a pair of thick gloves and a warm hat into her suitcase but she had packed with such a fuzzy brain and complete lack of her usual attention to detail. Never mind. In this climate, there was bound to be a shop selling woollens.

Because of the enticing spicy aromas floating from indoors as she passed the bakery, Hannah shelved resistance and bought a pastie and a takeaway cup of tea. All the indoor tables were full, so she strolled across to the shelter of the rotunda in the park, sitting in a sheltered pool of warming sunshine as she ate.

Rather than lug her groceries around, she decided to visit The Stables first. Taking up Will's recommendation, she located the huge old brick former stable building. The double doors with their wide metal triangular hinges were open and the sum streamed in through a row of skylights. Individual traders were set up in what were once the horse stalls, all now renovated to become pocket sized alcoves crammed with all possible manner of crafts. Hannah admired and envied them all. She was not at all creative. But then when had she ever sat still long enough to learn or become interested in any of these beautiful creative wares by clearly gifted artisans?

Hannah kept an eye out for Will's friend Emma and her jewellery stall. After losing track of time, absorbed in browsing, she eventually found her and discreetly approached. The attractive brunette, pliers in hand and wearing fingerless gloves, was head down and bent over her work table creating a delicately pretty necklace. She looked up as Hannah moved closer and smiled.

'Good afternoon. Are you looking for something special or happy to browse?'

'I'm Hannah Charles. Staying in St. Anne's.'

'Oh, of course. You're in the Lane,' Emma beamed and jumped to her feet. 'Your English accent is a right giveaway. I'm so pleased you introduced yourself.'

'Will recommended I come and take a look.'

'Did he now?' Emma grinned.

Hannah's gaze wandered over the glittering unique pieces in the glass counter cases or dripping with colour and reflected light on display trees.

'Your work is all gorgeous. My youngest sister Chelsea would love any of these.'

'Thank you.'

Filled with excitement over a spot of totally indulgent shopping and in female heaven at the array of beautiful treasures, Hannah decided to buy each of her sisters gifts of jewellery to take back to England. Based on her descriptions of her siblings, whose tastes and favourite colours she knew so well, Emma helped her choose three sets of matching necklaces and earrings.

As she carefully boxed and wrapped them, Emma said, 'I hope you're settling in. I guess it will take a while.'

'I've already met Will and Alma, and now you, so meeting folk is easy enough.'

'Since it's a holiday, you'll have plenty of time for relaxing and sightseeing.'

Hannah groaned. 'That's the issue. Filling in my time for three months. I'm learning my problem is sitting still.'

Emma laughed. 'Sounds like a wonderful dilemma to have.'

'Truth to tell I haven't missed my work at all. Which is really saying something because I lived and breathed it back home.'

Emma glanced up from tying each jewellery box with ribbon and popping them into one of her small labelled store bags.

As she placed them on the counter, she asked, 'What's your line of work?'

'Accountant.' Hannah wrinkled her nose. 'Boring in comparison to all this. You're so talented. I could never do anything so creative.'

'You might surprise yourself.'

Hannah sighed. 'Doubtful. Do you work here every day?'

Emma nodded. 'Busiest on weekends so I use week days like today for assembling pieces or working on new designs.'

'Are you a born and bred local?'

'Yes. Will and I attended primary school together but I moved away with my family to Sydney and his went to Melbourne. I returned occasionally to visit my gran, Mary Hamilton. She's a lifetime Tingara resident, volunteers in the op shop among many other things. Then last year my marriage failed and I returned to Tingara here as though I'd never left. At the time I needed that sense of familiarity I guess. The easy pace of small town life. More people should do it.' She smiled. 'Good for the soul. I'm divorced now. Starting again. My fiancé Mal Webster is a builder. He and Will are working on a building development project together actually. Mal has a six year old son, Daniel, from a previous relationship. He's from Bendigo originally. His parents and Daniel's mother still live there. So he often commutes back and forth. Daniel visits every other weekend. Wonderful having a child around the house. He's made me broody for children of my own.'

It was impossible not to notice the warmth that had crept into Emma's voice when she spoke of the two special men in her life. 'Do you have family still in Sydney?'

'My parents and a married sister. My nomadic young brother, Richard, is still single and lives up on the north coast. It's probably early days yet but, based on what you've seen so far, are you glad you took the plunge to come out here?'

Hannah considered the question, reviewing her first days and impressions. 'Well I guess if I hadn't stuck my finger on a map,' she admitted, 'I would never have come. I've never left England. Only done short holiday trips around the UK and Europe with girlfriends and my sisters.' Long before she became a workaholic, engrossed with work and caring for her parents. 'Not recently though.'

'Sounds like you deserve this holiday then.'

Did she? Hannah never thought of herself as deserving.

'Call around to our place any time. The old bluestone blacksmith's cottage down by the creek.'

'I must go walking and explore further then. I'll let you get back to your work while I brave the outdoors again. I can't believe I forgot to pack a hat and gloves,' she laughed at herself.

'Pop down to the op shop further along Main Street. Turn right when you leave here. Gran's there today. Ask for Mary. Introduce yourself and give her my love. They have heaps of beautiful hand knits. You might find something.'

'Thanks. Cheers.'

So Hannah found herself back out in the cold and tramping further down the street, grateful she'd worn her thickest jumper, leggings under her jeans and long leather boots. The op shop was easily found because of the sandwich board under the veranda out front. From Emma's description, her Gran was easily found stacking donated books on shelves. Chatty and sprightly, after introductions, she ushered Hannah to the knits section where she chose a floppy angora knitted beret with a matching scarf and a pair of soft wool-lined leather gloves.

'Pink suits you, dear,' Mary said.

'I wish I could knit. I'd love to make something like this but I'm sure I'd be all fingers and thumbs.'

'You're staying opposite Alma Powell in the Lane. She's in the CWA. A champion knitter and baker. She'll teach you.'

'What's the CWA?'

'Country Women's Association. Large voluntary women's organisation. Not unlike your Women's Institute in England I should say.'

Hannah brightened. 'My mother was in the WI.' And felt an ache at the reminder.

Maybe one day - far distant in the future she was sure - she would actually be able to think and speak of her parents with genuine peace and fond nostalgia. Instead of this awful sense of dread at even the thought of them gone now or mention of their names.

'Are you all right, dear?' Mary was speaking.

Upset by unwanted memories, she said, 'Yes. Thank you.' Distracted, she swiftly paid for her clothes. 'Don't bother wrapping. I'll wear them.'

Snug with the beret pulled over her long trailing hair, the scarf tightly wound about her neck and gloves warming her icy fingers, Hannah hurried to the small supermarket. She cursed the unwelcome flashbacks that randomly popped into her mind without warning.

She grabbed a trolley and pushed it around the aisles as though it was a weapon, whipping what she needed off the shelves before striding back down the Lane to St. Anne's with an armful of plastic carrier bags, feeling miserable, with an urgency and tightness in her chest to hibernate again. Well it *was* winter, she muttered to herself, trying for some feeble humour.

She retreated to the chapel's sanctuary, sending up prayers to be left alone. Hopefully, this being a former church and all, they would be answered.

It took a while of muttering to herself but Hannah already knew she must not let her paranoia spoil her holiday nor let her life sink into a shambles. *Get a grip.*

She flung back the soft rug and rose from the sofa where she had curled into a ball of self-pity. She unpacked her groceries and tossed a chicken, noodle and vegetable stir fry into Ginny's electric wok. Then sat on the sofa watching telly and eating her dinner from a bowl with a fork.

Too much time on her hands and solitude would be her downfall if she didn't fight her demons. Starting tomorrow. After a long soaking bath to relax, dipping into that book she started reading and a good night's sleep, she would rectify her present brooding situation. She had been able to partly bury it back home in England beneath a mountain of work. Here, the very peace and liberty she craved made her vulnerable and exposed, a situation that became apparent soon after her arrival. Since conquering jet lag and the worst of her virus, her mind was sharp again, creating its own dilemma.

In the coming months, she decided to use her leisure to seriously consider the changes she needed to make in her life. How to move forward. Preferably without the emotional and mental load she had allowed to settle heavily on her shoulders.

Step one was working on that.

Chapter 4

Next morning, Hannah tried to remember how Will had made his porridge. Surprising herself, she took a random guess at the amounts and tossed the ingredients into a saucepan. Her trial result was more than acceptable. Impossible not to think of Will as she ate; the shambles of his physical surroundings yet the ease and pull of his company.

Rugged up and out walking later on a recce about town, Hannah's heart missed a beat when the man of her thoughts at breakfast walked toward her across the central town park. With his head down and deep in thought, he didn't notice her but perhaps becoming aware of another human being approaching, he looked up. The flare of hunger on his face took her by surprise and filled her with heat despite the cold.

He looked dishy but her mind rebelled against the vision of his sloppy track pants, hooded jumper, beanie pulled down low over his forehead and ears with the ends of his long hair showing beneath, and a thick scarf knotted at his neck.

'Morning,' she said brightly. 'Not painting yet?'

'Seeking inspiration.'

'Doesn't always come easily?'

'Depends on the circumstances.

His familiar drilling stare took her breath away. 'I tried your porridge this morning,' she gabbled nervously.

'Stick to your ribs?' he teased, his mood lighter.

'Hope so. I'm off exploring.'

'You have Ginny's car. Lots to see further out.'

Reluctant to drive, Hannah wondered how she would manage. Nightmare enough forcing herself to get into Ginny's little sports job clinging desperately to the wheel and crawling along the highway at night to get to Tingara.

'What do you recommend?' she crossed her fingers and asked. Maybe she could join a day tour.

'You could hire a bike and ride around the vineyards. Drive up into the Alps. Snow any day now. Go fishing.'

She guessed he tossed that last one in for fun. She wrinkled her nose and shook her head.

'Not your thing?' he paused. 'You could wait for a sunny day and come out painting with me.'

'Oh. Sure.' His offer caught her off guard. 'Where do you go?'

'I have some secret places,' he murmured.

'What would I do?'

'Relax. Read a book. Watch the natural world go about its business.'

'Okay.' She shrugged, surprising herself by such random agreement. 'Let me know.'

'If you ever feel like some slow-paced independent adventures, you're welcome to borrow my ancient but fairly reliable bike. Fresh air will whip up some colour into those pale cheeks of yours.'

He always noticed such personal things about her. 'They're white this morning because I'm frozen,' she chuckled.

He strolled past her to move on. Half turning back, he said, 'I'll wheel my treadly up to St. Anne's anyway and leave it by the porch. Lots of tourist trails in the area for cyclists.'

'All right but I can't promise I'll use it. I haven't ridden since university in Oxford.'

'Enjoy your day,' he drawled and left.

'You too,' she called after him.

What was happening here, she wondered in alarm as she walked on, longing to look back but afraid?

She regrouped her thoughts and strode on with purpose out along the creek in search of Emma's cottage. Having found it, she stopped by the timber arch in the front fence. It looked old, built in dark grey slabs so different to the honey golden stone houses of the Cotswolds. It was charmingly small though with the central front door painted bright red and small paned windows either side.

Forced by the sharp air to keep moving, Hannah followed a gravelled trail along a bush lane closely hugged by woodland, with always the gurgling music of the creek somewhere off to her left. At the end, the track suddenly opened out onto a street again. She loved their names. She was staying in Gum Tree Lane and, according to the sign post, this one was Wattle Gully Road.

Heading back toward the centre of town she passed a gracious old white weatherboard home with verandas all around. A name plate by the gate in the white picket fence said *Clovelly*.

Passing fellow walkers, joggers and cyclists, some elderly Hannah noted with admiration, she acknowledged the simple and – in her life at least – forgotten pleasure of walking. Back home it was always a means to an end, rushing to catch a train or make the office on time. She figured her stroll this morning had probably been half an hour plus stopping to chat briefly to Will and take the occasional photos on her phone.

She loved rambling. As children, she and her sisters had disappeared for hours over summer holidays and weekends in the surrounding hills. She always fancied undertaking more of The Cotswold Way running along the escarpment of the hills from Chipping Campden all the way south down to gorgeous Bath. Apparently 100 miles of magical walking. But of course she had never made the time or effort to accomplish it.

But as refreshing as it was, although freezing, to have nothing better to do than walk, read, eat and sleep, and feeling better for it since those first confined days in town, she knew she needed something *more* to occupy her three months here. The endless idle weeks stretched ahead like a burden rather than a gift. She didn't want to go home, and couldn't. Ginny was in her cottage. She was anchored here. Tingara certainly wasn't the worst place in the world to have chosen. In fact, the village was pleasantly bucolic, and the locals seemed friendly.

Reaching the main street again, Hannah passed the bakery. Assailed by the sweet yeasty smells coming from inside, she flunked resistance and ducked inside for a small seeded wholemeal loaf and sticky iced fruit scrolls.

As she turned the corner into Gum Tree Lane, she literally collided with Alma, trudging purposefully uphill, a string shopping bag over one arm. They smiled and murmured apologies to each other.

Before moving off again, Hannah said, 'Alma?' She hesitated. Should she impose and ask or not? 'Mary Hamilton mentioned you might be able to teach me how to knit.'

Alma puffed out her chest, trying to look

indignant. 'Oh, she did now, did she?'

Hannah cringed, hoping there wasn't some issue between the two women she couldn't possibly know about. 'She said you were the best,' she hinted hopefully.

'Did she now?' Alma's annoyance turned to hesitant pleasure. 'Well. All right then. But I'm busy, mind. I'll have to see when I can fit you in.'

Hannah smiled to herself. 'Wonderful. Thank you so much for helping me. Just let me know when it suits. I'll fit in with your schedule.'

Alma wavered. 'I suppose we could try for an evening. Tonight or tomorrow. I don't have any meetings.'

'Great. I would appreciate that. Tonight after dinner?' Hannah offered.

Alma regarded her for such a long moment, she wondered if she'd been too eager and blown her welcome but then the older woman's manner softened. 'I'm putting a shepherd's pie in the oven tonight. Come for tea and we can share it.'

'Oh Alma, how lovely. Thank you. About six?'

'Come earlier if you like and we can indulge in a small glass of sherry first,' Alma leaned closer and confided as though they might be overheard.

'Wonderful,' Hannah pretended to be enthusiastic.

Knitting would be an experiment for sure, although she would probably be all thumbs with the wool but it would be so nice to share a meal again instead of eating alone. So far, since being in Tingara she had only shared a cup of tea with Will. Although instead of sherry, she would have preferred a glass of red. Well, pink really. She loved rosé. As they waved and parted, Hannah suspected there was something more behind Alma's bluster. Like a forced pretence. Covering up what exactly, she wondered?

On impulse, she returned to the small liquor section in the grocery store and bought a bottle of her favourite wine. She would take it over to Alma tonight. If she drank sherry, she might consider this, too. She gave the impression of being a cheerful but private person.

Back at St. Anne's, Hannah noticed Will had wasted no time and already delivered his bike, propped up against the porch. He was right. It had clearly cycled better days but his offer was thoughtful and generous. She would need a trial practise run up and down the Lane first before she ventured further afield though.

Hoping no one was out to witness her first wobbly efforts, Hannah pedalled easily down the Lane, turned around at the bottom and came back up the rise again. She longed to duck into Will's house and boast of her new balance and confidence but his shed was empty and his car missing.

Deflated with disappointment, she cycled back home, rugged up in her new beret and scarf, tossed a bottle of water and a snack into the wicker basket and left. She had studied a map and folded it safely in her shoulder bag with her mobile phone fully charged against any emergency.

She found the right road out of town and headed into the countryside, thankfully reasonably flat. Her heart lifted with the peace and freedom of a sunny but fresh day. She found the steady motion of pedalling blanked her mind and the sheer pleasure of the easy exercise exhilarating. The breeze tugged back her long hair from beneath her beret so that it streamed out behind.

The particular cycling trail she chose was well sign posted and led firstly to the rustic buildings of a farmhouse cheese factory and café. She decided to brave eating out on the vine-wrapped outdoor terrace, bare overhead without leaves, of course, but blessed with drenching sun today as she sat in a sheltered corner.

Her cheese platter lunch served with seasonal fruits, nuts and the farm's own fresh baked sourdough bread, was a sample tasting of their produce, all made, she learned, with fresh milk from local cows and goats that grazed the lush pastures of both the valleys and high country.

The creamy soft blue cheese married perfectly with a ripe pear. When she finished, Hannah lingered over the last mouthfuls of wine, equally savouring the view overlooking the emerald green winter landscape. Eventually and reluctantly, she forced herself to continue or she might not make it back to the village before the onset of another winter night.

Next stop was only another fifteen minute cycle to a winery where she sampled sparkling Shiraz and purchased two bottles to take home. Last call for the day was a chocolate shop tucked away on the roadside in a gorgeous but tiny stone building oozing homespun charm inside. Impossible to resist either buying or eating the decadent decorated truffles, so Hannah didn't bother. She bought a box for Alma and two more just because.

Cycling back into Tingara in the swiftly cooling weak late afternoon winter sunshine, Hannah realised her outing had been invigorating but perhaps a tad empty. Gripped by the heavy feeling of not so much being lonely as a sense of being alone. It would have been so much more fun had it been shared with another. Back home in England, she had deliberately covered her friendless life with work and family, making her barely aware of the void it created. All induced, of course, by the fateful events of twelve months prior.

Today, seeking the need of company again, she defied possible embarrassment and rode past St. Anne's, continuing on down the Lane to

Will. His contraption was in the shed. He was home. She cycled down his driveway to the back door. She hoped she wasn't interrupting his painting or presuming more of their friendship than he had already indicated. There was a spark between them. No denying. But being on holiday, Hannah had already given herself a strong lecture about keeping her distance. Will had simply been welcoming as all Tingara locals had been so far and he had lent his bike. No harm in a quick thank you.

He appeared with stealthy speed through the open French door and emerged out onto the patio before she had even parked the bike. Barefoot, hands sunk carelessly into his jeans, paint specks on his long sleeved tee shirt, and standing in the last small pool of sunlight that bleached the colour of his sandy hair, he grinned.

'Saw the bike gone. How was it?'

Well, at least he was pleased to see her and this morning's tension at their encounter in the park was missing, thank goodness.

'My legs are shaking from the effort,' Hannah admitted, strolling wearily closer. She peered over his shoulder to the sunroom behind. 'Did you find that inspiration you lost this morning?'

He nodded. 'Eventually.'

'Working on your landscape?'

'No. It's done.'

'I'd love to see it sometime.'

'Maybe,' he grinned. 'Where did you go today?'

She briefly explained her day, aware throughout her account of Will's gaze focused intently upon her as always. But for this once she bathed in his regard and fully embraced its warmth instead of her usual tendency to discomfort.

'So you had a great day then?'

She had nothing to fear from Will. He could become a good friend while she was here. So she found the admission that flowed from her mouth easier to voice. 'To be honest, it was interesting but…solitary. I guess I'm usually what most people might label a workaholic and therefore a loner. But commuting on the train, working in a busy office, you don't notice. Weekends were crammed with shopping, cleaning, babysitting my nephews or on the phone listening to my sisters' tragic clothes and boyfriend woes. There was always something happening.'

'Do you avoid your own company perhaps?' he asked bluntly.

Hannah bristled with defence. 'Not deliberately. That I'm aware of.'

'Be kind to yourself, Hannah,' he murmured.

His softly voiced warning let her know he was far more deeply aware and perceptive of her feelings than she realised. 'I believe I am.'

The intimacy of their comfortable

conversation evaporated with his cautionary advice.

'I best be off. I have dinner and a knitting lesson with Alma.'

'Tread carefully with her Hannah.'

She paused, frowning as she returned to the bike. 'Yes. Of course. Why wouldn't I?''

He nodded. 'She's had a hard life.'

'I'm sorry to hear it.'

Knowing his neighbour well, she respected his protective comment and almost felt bad for her curiosity over Alma's reserve.

Feeling reprimanded, Hannah turned the bike to cycle away when Will said, 'Emma and Mal and I, and sometimes our mate, Nick - with or without his boys - swap houses for dinner every few weeks when it suits everyone. It's my turn to play host next weekend. You're welcome to join us.'

Hannah still stung from his reproofs and asked sharply, 'Is that an invitation or an enquiry of my interest?'

If he could be blunt so could she. Always looking so damned humble and attractive even as he rebuked her. Where did he get off being so self-righteous? Who appointed him caretaker of everyone's emotions?

'An invitation.'

'All right,' she said half-heartedly. 'Let me know how I can contribute.'

Something to anticipate but certainly not for

the anticipation of Will's company alone, she decided, as she pedalled away.

Chapter 5

Always afraid of being late, Hannah strode across the Lane to Alma's cottage a good five minutes before six, clutching her box of truffles and bottle of wine. She let herself through the latched gate in the front picket fence and marched up to the door, her brief knock swiftly answered.

'Lovely. Right on time, dear.' Alma greeted her in a neat housedress and short embroidered cardigan, all covered by a full apron.

The gifts of chocolates and wine were bashfully accepted as though Alma was unaccustomed to receiving any.

'You might have need of the wine after you try to teach me to knit,' Hannah tried to lighten the mood.

Alma always seemed so serious, as though burdened. Bearing Will's warning in mind, Hannah determined not to pry. A virtual stranger's life was none of her business anyway but the older woman's tendency to brightness seemed forced.

Ushered into a cosy living room cluttered with old furniture and warmed by a flickering open fire, the promised sherry was poured and thrust into Hannah's hand.

'I'll just check on everything in the kitchen. Tea is ready.'

'Can I help?' Hannah called out after her as she disappeared.

'No dear. You warm up by the fire while I serve.'

She sauntered around the room, peering at the few small framed photographs on the mantelpiece. She noticed none were recent. She recognised a younger and trimmer Alma in a wedding gown with gorgeous wide lacy sleeves and a circlet of flowers holding a long wispy veil. She stood solemnly, arms linked, with her suave husband. Quite a handsome catch with his hair slicked back. 1970s she guessed, about her own parents' era of marriage.

The only other photo alongside it was of three school aged boys. That was all. No other later family portraits. She might have expected her sons' weddings perhaps and possibly grandchildren photos but there were none. Alma reappeared, flushed, whether from her sherry or cooking, Hannah couldn't say.

She caught Hannah's focus on the photographs as she stood in the doorway but ignored it and said quickly, 'Tea's ready. We'll eat at the kitchen table.'

'Lovely. I'm looking forward to your pie. I love your wedding dress,' Hannah added as she pulled out a chair at the small square table set precisely with china and cutlery, plates of food already in place.

She sighed. 'I still have it but it means nothing to me now. It was all so long ago.' Flustered, Alma said, 'Did you want to open your wine?'

'Only if you'll share with me.'

'All right then. Just a splash.'

'I'll do the honours if you like.'

'Might be wise. I rarely drink wine.' Alma placed the opened bottle and two old fashioned etched wine glasses before Hannah.

She poured and made a toast. 'To knitting.'

'And good food,' Alma managed a small grin as they clinked glasses.

'And friendship?'

'Indeed, dear.'

Hannah glimpsed a damp sparkle in Alma's eyes, obviously touched by the sentiment. So as not to embarrass her further, Hannah looked down and eagerly began her meal.

'Smell's delicious. I've already experienced Will's soup and tried his porridge, although he never seems to bother with a recipe.'

'That's because he's a naturally gifted cook. And he experiments. My goodness, what concoctions that young man doesn't throw together. I've memorised all my favourite recipes and still use them. Do you like to cook, dear?'

'I've never had much time after I finish work and travel home.'

'That's a pity.'

'My mother was a wonderful country cook. I have all her recipe books. Just never got around to using them really.'

'So she's passed on then, your mother?' Alma prompted gently.

Hannah swallowed against the rising lump in her throat. 'Yes, both my parents are gone now.'

'I'm sorry to hear that, dear. It's clear you miss them.'

Was it so obvious? Hannah nodded.

'Do you have brothers or sisters?' Alma went on.

'Three sisters. All younger than me in their twenties and thirties,' she managed between mouthfuls of pie and sips of wine. 'Heather's married and I often babysit her sons. The two youngest live in London.'

'But you keep in touch.'

'Yes, we do.'

'That's nice.'

'I noticed the photo of three boys in your sitting room. Your sons?'

'Yes.' Alma paused and stared across the room. 'I rarely see them nowadays now though.'

'They don't come to visit?' Hannah wondered if she was treading on that forbidden ground but Alma seemed content to talk.

'No, dear. I don't drive and they all live in the city. The wives work, too.' She wrinkled her nose. 'They're all a bit starchy for me. We've little in common. I'm considered old fashioned, doing baking and crafts and gardening but it's what I love and have done all my life.'

Hannah drew in a deep breath and asked, 'Grandchildren?'

'Five. Apparently.' Alma laid down her cutlery neatly across her finished meal, her quiet response a combination of regret and disapproval.

How cruel. Hannah ached on her behalf that, for whatever reason – the family's distance or disharmony and perhaps even apathy – aging parents were sometimes neglected. She could never have imagined not having her own folks in her life, having moved jobs and cities to care for them. The least Alma's sons could do, she would have thought, was keep in contact with their mother or send photographs. She would bet Alma didn't own a computer but telephones and snail mail still worked.

Fascinated and sad for her, Hannah longed to ask about Alma's husband but the poor woman had voiced enough disappointment for one night, she suspected. She would leave their conversation there. This, she was sure, was the very reason Will cautioned her against curiosity.

'More wine?' Hannah asked.

'It's rather lovely, dear. I believe I will.'

She gathered their empty plates, took them to the sink and rinsed then, stacking them neatly to one side. 'I've made us some little baked custards for dessert.'

As Alma set a small jug of cream between them, Hannah admired with pleasure and memories her own mother's cooking when the small round dish liberally topped with nutmeg was set down before her.

'Do start. It's nothing fancy.'

From the first mouthful, the light creamy still-warm dessert melted in Hannah's mouth. She didn't stop eating until she was scraping the ramekin clean.

'Alma that was delicious.'

'Simple enough to make. I'll jot down the recipe for you.'

Hannah was beginning to realise exactly how much she was taking away from this holiday already. 'I can photograph it on my mobile,' she suggested.

'Really? Whatever you think.'

Alma produced a battered old exercise book bulging with handwritten and pasted in recipes. When she opened it to the correct page, Hannah snapped it with her phone while Alma piled the dishes into the sink, ran in hot water and a squirt of wash liquid.

'I'll help you.' Hannah rose.

'No dear. We'll let them soak. Come into the lounge while the kettle boils and we'll get you started with some wool.'

'I hope you're big on patience,' Hannah chuckled as she followed.

'With a husband like mine,' Alma muttered, 'if you didn't have any you soon got some.'

'Oh, dear,' was the only trite non-committal response Hannah could manage.

They settled on the old fashioned aged but comfy sofa together in front of the glowing burnt down coals pushing decent warmth out into the room. Alma produced wool and needles, made mugs of tea when the kettle sang and they settled down to work.

Hannah found it strangely comforting chatting to Alma in low tones as the older woman showed and patiently explained how to hold the wool and needle between her fingers, and the casting on process.

'You're making a scarf and it's all in simple garter stitch,' she announced.

Hannah's tea grew cold while Alma sipped hers, encouraged and supervised alongside until Hannah proudly held up her base row and began the repetitive movements of knitting back and forth. It reminded her of the times, mainly in winter, after she had returned home to live in the family cottage in Snowshill with her parents when she sat down beside her mother, the older woman's knitting needles softly clicking, for a last refreshing cuppa and chat in front of the fire before bed and another early morning commute and busy weekday. Hannah found it as companionable being with Alma. Regarding the homely older person beside her brought a wistful lump to her throat but she suppressed it.

From Alma's quick reference earlier to her husband, Hannah couldn't help wondering about him, the suave man smiling down at them from the photo on the mantel. Even as she dwelt on the mystery, Alma started talking again.

'Do you have a boyfriend, dear?'

'No time really,' Hannah confessed and stopped knitting for a moment in reflection.

'A pretty thing like you? Such a shame.' Alma clucked her tongue. 'Will's a nice young man. Bit wild for Tingara I thought at first, coming back like he did a few years ago but he's settled and built that lovely house. He's talented, that's for sure and a good catch,' she hinted, staring into the fire.

'I hope you're not suggesting a holiday romance, Alma,' Hannah teased.

'Why ever not?' she retorted, her mouth edged with humour.

She scoffed. 'You know I live in England. Besides, I'm not in the market for a chap. Blast. I dropped a stitch.' Just thinking of their neighbour down the Lane unsettled her.

Alma fixed it and Hannah continued knitting.

'He's a good man, young Will. He's been like a son to me.' She leaned closer. 'He's not real close to his family, though.'

'He mentioned. Do you know why?'

'High and mighty, I think. Opposite of Will. I remember the family from years ago.' Alma gazed into the fire again, mesmerised as one tended to be by the shapes of flames leaping about.

'The father was always aiming higher. You could see Tingara wasn't enough for him. Smart suits. Man of few words. Started his own legal practice. After he married a big local landowner's daughter, they only stayed a few years, hobnobbed with the town's best. Had their own elite social circle but moved away to the city while the children were all still young. He studied for the bar then I heard and now he's an important successful barrister. Often see him in the news fighting big legal cases.'

Alma turned back to Hannah. 'Will's nothing like them at all. He's much too down to earth. Hard to imagine him being their son really.' She checked Hannah's progress. 'You're doing well there. Half a dozen rows already. You'll have a scarf in no time.' She rose and gathered up their mugs. 'I'll make you another cuppa and we'll dip into those chocolates you brought.'

After they had drunk, eaten and chatted a while longer, Alma disappeared, returning to produce some of her own beautiful hand knits.

Hannah gasped. 'Alma they're gorgeous. How long does this take you?' She fingered the raised patterns of a thickly soft neutral coloured jumper.

'An Aran design like that a few weeks or a month working on it most evenings.'

'I can see now why Mary recommended you. I'm learning from the best. But don't expect me to produce anything like this,' she laughed.

'I made one for Will in a similar colour to match those lovely brown eyes of his.'

'Are they?'

Hannah pretended she hadn't noticed but, of course, they were one of many arresting features belonging to the wildly enticing and enigmatic man. How did *he* suddenly become the centre of their conversation again?

By her own admission, Alma clearly held a fondness for Will but Hannah also held the suspicion it might also be with the intention to bring him to her attention. No need really. She had already succumbed to his unconventional appeal.

Sneaky old dear, Hannah smiled to herself. Not knowing Will well enough yet, why on earth did Alma believe they would suit each other? Maybe she was just a born matchmaker. She wouldn't have thought her a romantic at heart because Hannah sensed her own marriage had been unhappy. There was no sign of Mr. Powell anywhere.

Alma meant well, Hannah supposed, but it served no purpose. Will Bennett was a nice enough chap for sure but she was only here on holiday and lived on the other side of the world.

As a diversion, she asked, 'Do those Aran patterns mean anything?'

'I don't believe there's any particular truth behind the stitches. It depends on who you ask and it's all to do with the sea but it's said that the cable represents the fishermen's ropes. The lattice supposedly represents their baskets, the diamonds can symbolise the island fields or fishing nets. The truth is, there's no real authentic meanings. They were created for their decorative appeal by clever knitters. All the same, interesting to speculate.'

'I guess so.' Hannah held up the small length of her first humble knitting effort. 'Makes mine look rather ordinary.'

'You're doing fine. Take your work home with you and keep working on it. You'll find it therapy while you're achieving something.'

Besides her love of it, Hannah wondered if that was part of the reason Alma knitted. 'How did you learn?'

'Self-taught. Always been attracted to the softness and textures of different wools, and their colour combinations. While I was raising a family, it was all cooking and housework and knitting for the boys out of necessity really. When *he* left,' Alma nodded toward the wedding photograph, 'I went out to work. I was behind the bakery counter for years. Did sewing and knitting for people in the evenings, catered food for functions on weekends. It all helped to put the boys through school.

'As soon as they finished secondary, they couldn't wait to leave for the city. They've all done well, though, I'll give them that. Put themselves through university. A credit to them all really with no father about as a role model.'

'Sounds like you took on that part admirably all by yourself.' Hannah paused. Should she? 'Where is he now?'

'Could be dead for all I know or care. Swept a naïve country girl like me off my feet, married me, got me pregnant three times then disappeared.' She sighed. 'I've thought about trying to trace him over the years, find out more, but what purpose would it serve now? At least he left me with a roof over my head even if it came with a mortgage.'

'You've never tried to find him?'

Alma shook her head. 'Never wanted to really.'

'Never wondered?'

'Oh, of course I did, dear, but he treated me so unkindly I was glad to see the back of him. I don't ever want to see his face again. I hope he had a rotten life.'

Hannah reached out and gently laid a hand on Alma's arm, understanding now what Will meant about her hard life, humbled that the older woman trusted her enough to confide. Not necessary when she was only here for a few months.

Because Hannah keenly felt the loss of her own parents and especially her mother, she cherished this woman's friendship and desperately wished she could do something – anything – to help. But what? Alma seemed content enough here in her own small place in the world. Tingara was familiar. It was home. And, to her credit, Alma didn't appear to be the kind of woman who dwelt on the hand life had dealt her.

All the same, she could throttle those three sons and their families for distancing themselves from this dear woman who had worked hard all her life and probably never harmed anyone yet, in fact, had harm done to her. Hannah would be willing to bet Alma raised her boys to be better than their father. From her own account, she had given her all to them and now received little in return. Where was their humanity, if not gratitude?

It was after eleven when Hannah hugged Alma at her front door and dashed back across the Lane in the still and nippy air. Alma sent her home with more balls of wool and the partly-started garter stitch scarf to practice. If she ever managed to finish, it would be a useful addition to her winter woollies and cherished memento of her friendship with Alma and holiday in Tingara.

Still bothered while she snuggled under the

doona and before she could fall asleep for thinking about Alma and her life, Hannah now knew her temporary neighbour's brittle attitude on first acquaintance was to stop people getting too close. No doubt damaged by her innocently poor choice of husband and his desertion some years later.

The attached stigma, gossip and shock for Alma that surely followed at the time must have been enormous. Yet she had remained in Tingara and raised her sons alone in the face of it all. People like Will taking her into their hearts and lives. Hannah wondered what other close friends Alma claimed. Emma's gran, Mary, was of the same generation.

The pretended cheerfulness and busyness were fronts against a loneliness she would never admit.

Alma's isolated family situation bothered Hannah. She longed to do something, then pulled back from her tendency to take others' problems on board as though they were her own responsibility. This holiday was supposed to be getting away from and addressing all that in her life.

Hannah continued to toss and turn for a while. Unable to sleep she retrieved her iPad and checked her mail. As soon as she opened the one from her youngest sister, Chelsea, she realised this may be a huge mistake. What now?

Appalled by what she read, she checked the

time. It would be mid Saturday afternoon back home. Should she call? Chels could be out anywhere, shopping, socialising. She sent her a quick text instead. Within minutes her mobile rang.

'Chelsea this will be costing a fortune. Better make it fast.'

'No problem. I'm at home.'

'In London?'

'No!' she said impatiently. 'Mum and Dad's house.'

It wasn't theirs any more, of course. They were dead. It belonged to the four daughters now but they still referred to it in those former terms because, until last year, they had always known it so.

'Is Ginny there?' Hannah asked in alarm.

'Of course not.'

'How did you get in?'

'I still have my key, silly.'

'You were supposed to hand it in.'

She ignored her sister's reprimand and said, 'Hanny, I don't like the woman living in our house.'

'It's only for three months. She has the right and you knew all about it.'

'She says we're not to come around anymore.'

'I'm surprised you have. You rarely visit when I'm home. Why the sudden interest now?'

'Because you're gone.'

'How can that make a difference? What's the

point of visiting when I'm not there?'

'It doesn't. It's just knowing you're so far away.'

'Chels, you have to get out of that house. It's an invasion of Ginny's privacy whether she's there or not. I made a mutual agreement with her and explained it to you all before I left. I told you to take anything from the cottage you wanted so there would be no need for you to go back. You only have access now with Ginny's permission and with prior arrangement.'

'Oh bollocks to that.'

'You need to get off the phone. Hang up now and get out of there.'

'I don't want to. She's not here. She'll never know.'

'How do you know where she is?'

'At work, of course.'

'On a weekend?'

'Duh. She's exactly like you. It's all work work work with her, too.'

'You're snooping. If she finds out about this she'll be furious. She's a forceful personality.'

'I haven't touched a thing,' Chelsea objected.

'I hope not and don't go there again.'

'You're so bossy. It's all right for you with your university education and fancy job. You don't care about the rest of us.'

'I worked hard to go to Oxford. You could do the same.'

'Yeah, right. With whose money?'

'Your own. That you earn yourself. Like I did.' Hannah hadn't quite realised the extent of her younger sisters' reliance. From a distance, having stepped back in recent weeks, she now found the complaints and interruptions frustrating and intrusive. And shook her head that for the past year she had allowed herself to be so used.

As usual, Chelsea ignored her honesty and declared, 'Victoria's new boyfriend is getting really possessive and controlling.'

'She knows her own mind. I'm sure she can handle it herself. I can't do anything from over here. Can't you help? You're right there in the situation.'

'No! I'm seeing this hot new chap and I need to be available when he calls.'

'How can helping Victoria possibly affect that?'

'Just phone her please, Han. Give her advice.'

'No. It will cost a fortune.'

'You don't know the man,' Chelsea scoffed. 'He's old and rich.'

In that case, Hannah was surprised Victoria would even be interested but he must have been of some advantage to her when they met.

'Surely she can end the relationship if she wants. Tell him to sod off. She usually does to her menfolk when they no longer prove useful.'

'He's more powerful than that. I've met him once or twice at parties and he scares me.'

Gobsmacked by these selfish dramas, Hannah's patience thinned. Really? Victoria sounded like she was on with some geriatric mafia tosser. Chelsea had broken into their family home and was running up an astronomical bill even as they spoke. For which she herself may eventually end up being responsible if Ginny complained.

'Well all I can say is if Victoria puts herself out there she can live with the consequences.' Vic and Chelsea's social lives made Hannah look like a nun.

'You're so selfish,' Chelsea blasted. 'I don't know why I even bothered to ask. You don't care about us anymore and you won't help.'

'Why should I? You're all adults. You can look after yourselves. Go ask Heather. It's the middle of the night here. I have to get back to sleep. Bye Chelsea.'

Feeling empowered by her honesty, Hannah wondered why she'd never had this conversation before. Hopefully Chels would take her disinterest back to Vic and they sorted out their own problems. But that didn't stop her simmering fury that her sibling troubles had followed her to Australia. You would think that was far enough. Her next option was outer space!

How could two grounded women from a close family in a sleepy Cotswold village be so gormless? Heather survived unscathed by going down the traditional route of marriage to her high school sweetheart. But their two youngest sisters had wilful minds of their own and dramas followed them everywhere.

It was starting to look awfully tempting to simply turn off her phone or not recharge it. Disconnect herself from the world and social media. Often it was nothing but a nuisance anyway.

Her newfound inner peace these past weeks was still fragile enough to deteriorate again or be lost altogether. Being involved in her sisters' lives and turmoils again, mostly against her will, left her feeling freshly overwhelmed and anxious.

Hannah yawned, switched off her phone and the light. When Fluffy jumped up on the bed and settled across her feet, she fell asleep smiling.

Chapter 6

There was nothing else for it, Hannah argued with herself, and kept putting one foot in front of the other down the Lane to Will's place. It was now Tuesday. She hadn't seen him for days and he might not contact her until too late in the week. For her, that was *too* late. She needed to plan. Be organised. Shop for supplies. And not being much in the kitchen, she would probably need to do a trial run of the dish she chose for Saturday night's dinner.

She found Will on the sunny terrace sitting cross legged and straight backed on a mat, arms extended and resting gently on his knees. Meditating? She abruptly stopped but surely he must have heard her crunching footsteps approaching on the gravelled driveway.

What to do? Agonising seconds passed with fleeting thoughts of retreat but Will turned to her.

'Join me,' he said softly and patted the rug beside him.

There wasn't much room, Hannah noticed. It would be a close session.

'What am I supposed to do?' she whispered.

'You don't have to whisper,' he whispered back, teasing.

'I didn't want to spoil your quiet.'

'You already have,' he mocked, grinning.

'Sorry. I should have left.'

Hannah always felt like a bumbling idiot around Will. He was so lazily assured and had a way of making fun she found unnerving. The reason she realised was that she wanted him to think well of her. Like her. And she doubted, so far, that she measured up.

'You're here now. Sit down,' he urged again. 'Blank your mind. Absolutely no thoughts allowed. Slow deep breathing and just…be in the moment. Relax your mind and let go.'

Hannah settled down beside him.

'Comfortable?' he asked.

'Mm.'

'Okay. Just focus on your breathing or an object.'

What Hannah focused on at first was how alive she felt with Will so close alongside. Not exactly what he had instructed she knew, but how could she concentrate when she felt their shoulders touch and she could hear *his* steady breathing?

For starters she thought of everything. Her mind ran riot over her dinner and chin wag with Alma the other night, and all her disclosed revelations. How they waved to each other now across the Lane and how she nipped across to visit her cottage but Alma, strangely, never came to St. Anne's. Her sisters' dilemmas back home. What would eventuate on the rest of her holiday here in Tingara?

So it was hard, if not impossible, to find stillness. But slowly, eventually, her thoughts stopped churning long enough to become aware that the morning sun gaining strength now poured like remedial warm liquid through her body. The emerald and scarlet lorikeets she had come to recognise and appreciate as typical of the Australian bush screeched somewhere off in the distance.

A faint breeze teased back the ends of her hair. Amid an awareness of all these things in her surroundings, Hannah had no idea of time until Will spoke.

'All right?' he murmured.

'Are we done now?'

'If you want.'

'Not sure how successful I was. My mind raced for a while.'

'That's normal and a good sign actually.'

He sprang to his feet then held out a hand to help Hannah rise. She took it and he wrapped his firm grip to pull her up beside him.

'Thanks.'

She rubbed her hands together, remembering the warm feel of his skin against hers while he rolled up the mat and headed indoors.

'When did you start meditating?' she asked as he held the door open for her. 'And why?'

'In my surfing days. Some mates were doing it so I tried it.' He shrugged.

Will was a surfie? Made sense. Easy lifestyle and part of Australia's image and culture in the world but he wouldn't be catching any waves here in Tingara.

They wandered through the sunroom, a new landscape taking shape on the easel canvas, Hannah noticed. A few swipes of background colour, what looked like an horizon line and not much else. This one promised to be a larger work.

In the kitchen, Will poured two glasses of water and pushed one toward her.

'We're talking guys who worked out,' Will reverted to their meditating surfie conversation. 'Attuned to themselves physically and spiritually. I grew to admire and respect their adherence to a certain philosophy for lifestyle choice and balance. It's a part of my life now, too. You should try it regularly,' he suggested. 'It makes you aware how noisy your thoughts are but meditation is a gradual process. You learn to train your mind and make friends with it.'

Hannah leaned against the kitchen counter and sipped her water, fascinated by Will, his low voice, the dreamy look of him. She stared. He talked.

'These days,' he continued, 'people waste time and energy trying to find happiness, peace and satisfaction. They don't stop to ask themselves the real source. Within our own mind. Society offers us endless stuff claiming to make us happy or whatever but that only creates a hunger for more.'

'Sneaky commercialism,' Hannah agreed, deeply invested in what he was saying, intrigued by his principles and truth. Something to consider for her own life.

'Exactly. There are two kinds of happiness. Physical comfort which, in the western world most people achieve. And mental contentment. People concentrate on the outer wealth and neglect to make time for their inner needs.'

Hannah nodded madly. 'My life was crazy before I came here. I'm learning to slow down.'

The irony didn't pass unnoticed by her of that fateful finger poke on a Google map of the world and the subtle healing process that had begun for her in this tiny village of Tingara on the other side of the world.

'At sunrise my surfie mates might be sitting on the beach meditating or watching the sky change amazing colours.' He smiled to himself. 'Next thing they're pumping adrenalin riding monster waves back into shore.'

'Sounds like you've led an interesting life.'

'Not much use for my surfboard up here in the country. I get down to the coast when I feel the need. So, why did you come visit this morning?' he asked suddenly.

'Oh.' So easy to get side tracked around this chap. 'You hadn't contacted me yet about what to bring for dinner.'

'Plenty of time. We have until the end of the week.'

'I don't. I prefer to be organised.'

'I noticed.'

'Not a bad thing.'

'Fair enough,' he drawled, clearly holding back amusement. 'Short answer is, whatever you please. Entirely free choice.'

'What are you making? So I don't double up.'

'Won't know until Saturday when I check the vegie patch. Depends what's fresh and ripe on the day.'

'That's no help.'

'Like I said, it's up to you. If it's too hard, don't bring anything except your lovely self. There's always heaps of food.'

Hannah frowned. 'I'll think of something. I have Alma's shepherd's pie recipe. I could try that. Too ordinary?'

He didn't reply. Instead, he asked, 'How did your evening go with her?'

Hannah related their dinner then knitting and chat by the fire, and the extent of Alma's confidences.

'I didn't pry. She talked,' Hannah quickly defended.

'She doesn't trust nor make friends easily.' He regarded her steadily which she may have misread as admiration. Or not. She could drown in that velvety brown gaze.

'It was just passing references really but, I mean, what kind of husband just walks out on his wife and children?'

'A deadbeat usually. Would have been worse for her if he'd stayed.'

'Yes. Alma hinted. Did you know him?'

'Bernie?' Will shook his head. 'Don't remember him. Like you, I've only seen him in the wedding photo.'

'What was his work?'

'Farm labourer. Wasn't always employed either, I gather.'

'Do you know anything about her sons?'

'Inquisitive little thing, aren't you?' he mocked softly.

'Just interested.' She felt herself blush. Honestly, Will's stare gave her the collywobbles. Made her feel vulnerable. 'Alma's is a sad story.'

Will drummed his fingers on the counter and frowned in thought. 'Martin's the oldest I think, then Anthony and the youngest was Sam.'

Good solid names, Hannah reflected. 'They all live in Melbourne and do well, Alma said.'

'Yeah. Except they never visit.'

She nodded and a mini silence of contemplation stretched between them. Time she was moving on with her day. 'Thanks for the session out there. It was engrossing. I'll see you Saturday. What time?'

'When you're ready.'

Hannah sighed. She should know by now not to always expect a direct or definite answer from Will.

Probably seeing her frustration, he grinned and her heart lurched again. 'I'll be here.'

'Of course you will. See you Saturday. At a time of my choosing,' she added cheekily over her shoulder as she wandered back out through the sunroom. Cheers.'

She caught a glimpse of Will, hands thrust deeply into his baggy trouser pockets and a foxy smile on his face. How on earth was it even possible that this adorable untidy man did not have a woman in his house and bed?

As she walked home in the crisp air, her heart light and an extra spring in her step, Hannah reflected on Will's philosophies. An example to take on board in her own life? His attitude and lifestyle also explained why he always seemed so content, quiet even, and at ease with himself, others and his surroundings.

Comparing his life to her own there was heaps to admire. Will Bennett was so…together. For a chap, or a *bloke* as they said here in Australia. Clearly so far in her life in England she had only encountered wankers or been looking in the wrong places. It took a random holiday Down Under to shake up her attention to the facts.

Hannah didn't see Will for the rest of the week. Almost as though he deliberately avoided her but he *was* working on his exhibition. She was the one on holiday. She realised early on that she didn't have his phone number nor did he offer it. She could always visit him, drop in unexpectedly, put herself out there and let him know she was interested. Which she was but the idea totally blasted in the face of common sense when she was here only temporarily.

Besides, she wasn't a woman to chase chaps, let them know she was on the pull. Because she wasn't. Never had been. The one time she let herself go and moved too fast into a romance she regretted. The relationship with David was a disappointment and, soon, a disaster after the first weeks but they had struggled on for six months until both gasped with relief to end it.

Lesson learned. Let chaps chase *her*. If sparks flew, she would pay attention. Hannah sighed. Unfortunately or not, depending which way one looked at it and against all logic, Will Bennett fitted that category.

Despite having all week to prepare, Saturday threw her into a muddle. What to cook was sorted. On Alma's advice when she dashed yet again across the Lane two days ago for advice, she changed the topping on the shepherd's pie to pastry for a twist on traditional mash.

What to wear was another matter. She eyed

everything she had brought from England that she had unpacked and hung up in Ginny's wardrobe. Nothing looked a possibility. She had half a mind to wander down to the op shop and see if Mary had anything suitable. At Will's house, with a group of friends, she doubted it would be dressy. Will by nature would be informal. Whatever *he* wore would be loose and comfortable and he would look scrummy.

How to catch his eye? In the end, she opted for jeans, a long soft blue knitted top and boots, then crimped her hair but left it down and swinging free in waves.

She cursed Will's flexible arrival time and knew she would be early but by six she grew edgy to be off so she bundled up in a coat and scarf, loaded up the picnic basket she had found in the laundry cupboard with her steaming hot pie fresh from the oven, flaky pastry nicely risen thank you, a bottle of rosé and a box of chocolates.

Striding down the Lane in the bracing evening air, the starry night sky was a refreshing change from the past few dismal wet days. As though the rain had washed nature clean again. By the time the short walk brought her to Will's place, she felt calmer and determined to enjoy the evening despite being a newcomer, except for Will and Emma, mostly among strangers.

Fairy lights traced a path along the driveway to the rear terrace and French doors. She tapped on the glass pane and Mr. Wonderful appeared within moments. Hannah gaped, feeling like a school girl before a pop star. How wrong could you be?

Will's long hair fell from the centre in loose waves to his shoulders. No pony tail tonight but he hadn't forsaken his usual trademark bare feet. With a long sleeved black tee shirt pushed up to the elbows over tight fitting jeans, crumbs, how was she supposed to concentrate on anything tonight?

Even worse, he beamed at the sight of her, lighting up his face and eyes, transporting him from irresistible to dangerous. Whatever it was about this chap left her breathless and rattled.

'Hiya,' she grinned foolishly as he opened the door and took her basket. 'I'm early.'

'Perfect. Hoped you would be.'

He closed the door behind them, grasped her hand and led her through an unusually tidy sunroom and into the warm inviting kitchen alive with herby cooking aromas.

'Something smells wonderful.'

Callie obviously thought so too for she entwined herself around their ankles.

'Herbed Mediterranean vegetables. And a dessert.' He flipped off the tea towel cover Hannah had placed over her basket contents.

'Basically shepherd's pie without the spuds.'

He grinned. 'Looks amazing. The pastry is an inspired touch. I'll pop it into the oven to keep warm.'

As he bent to do so, Hannah mentally fanned herself against the vision of his tight arse, her mind completely out to lunch. She almost missed what he said next.

'Emma usually brings a salad and interesting savoury nibbles so the food sorts itself out really.'

Hannah smiled and nodded. It was all she could manage. Crumbs. She wanted to see what that messy hair of his felt like between her fingers. Flustered, she cast her gaze further afield over Will's shoulder and glimpsed something amazing in the dining room beyond.

He noticed the direction of her stare and said, 'Come through.'

All the while, his warm hand held hers, fingers firmly linked. Hannah grew alarmed by what was happening inside her and between them, as though a barrier had suddenly come down. She hadn't a clue what caused it to crumble but the consequences were scary. She wanted it to develop and yet she didn't. For a long list of very sensible reasons.

The large raw and rustic timber table looked as though it had been hewn from one giant tree trunk. Grouped fat white candles flickered already alight at its centre but Hannah's attention was drawn to the stunning art work on the opposite wall.

'Your work?' Will nodded. 'A mural.'

'Fresco actually. You apply paint directly to freshly plastered walls and when it sets, the painting becomes part of the wall.'

'How is a mural different?' Hannah turned to ask, so close their bodies brushed together from the shoulders all the way down.

'More work for a start. There are two stages. An underpainting first to block in the main areas and do a general composition outline. Then you paint the detail.'

They had moved around the table as he spoke so Hannah gently ran her hand over the image as they passed. Such a realistic Australian bush landscape, she felt as if she was a part of it. Will's touch of genius was the fact that he had framed it like a traditional painting hung on a wall.

'This is a cracking piece of work. You're so talented.'

'Thank you,' he murmured humbly. 'I've been splashing paint around all my life. I started by doing graffiti actually.'

Hannah raised her eyebrows. 'I thought that was illegal.'

Will grinned. 'It is.'

'Okay,' she replied slowly. There was a story in there somewhere she was sure but didn't dare pursue it and Will didn't either.

'Glad you're here early actually. I can give you a heads up on my friends coming tonight.'

'Brilliant.'

'You've met Emma of course down at The Stables. She and Mal are engaged to be married in spring and they live together in the old blacksmith's cottage down by the creek.'

'I've walked by. It's cute and gorgeous.' Like someone else she knew.

'Mal is a master builder and comes from Bendigo a few hours away. He has a five year old son Daniel from another relationship. The boy often spends the weekend with him and he'll be coming tonight.'

Much of this Emma had already mentioned but Will's explanations helped refresh the details in her mind.

'My nephews Andrew and James are a bit younger. Preschool still.'

'I'm collaborating with Mal on a sustainable green housing development on the edge of town. Further out Gum Tree Lane actually. What?' Will asked as Hannah grinned at him.

'You never cease to surprise me. You're such an easy going person, I wonder how you manage it all.'

'At my own pace. Whatever I do is my passion. We've bought the land, now we're in the process of creating an estate master plan. Doing surveys, planning infrastructure and the overall development in stages. Stony Creek winds through the far side of it so we've decided to call the project *Creekside*. The house designs will all be on the same principles as mine, passive solar.'

'I'm impressed. Who knew all this talent and enterprise existed in Tingara?'

They heard car doors slam and voices.

'Emma and Mal. She's usually the only female so she'll appreciate your company.'

'Is that why you invited me?' Hannah cringed even as she asked.

'Absolutely not,' Will drawled and kissed her tenderly on the cheek, yet close enough to the edge of her lips to leave her breathless.

'Before they come in I'll just mention Nick Logan and his boys. He's divorced. Rachel took off with a sugar daddy and left him to raise their sons alone.'

Hannah's heart twinged with compassion and she let a heavy sigh escape. 'Oh no,' she whispered.

'Tyler is the oldest, almost a teenager and off to secondary school next year. An angry kid unsurprisingly. Christopher is halfway through primary school and little Noah just started this year. Nick drive transports and works long hard hours. He can't always get a sitter for the boys when he needs to.'

'It might not be much help long term but I'm happy to help while I'm here,' Hannah offered. 'I often mind my nephews for my sister Heather and Michael so I've had some experience.'

'You should mention it tonight. Nick would appreciate it.'

'Websters are here,' a female voice called out.

Hannah followed Will back into the kitchen to greet them.

'You're not a Webster yet, Emma,' Will teased, kissing her on the cheek.

'I will be soon.' She looked over his shoulder. 'Hey Hannah. How's Tingara treating you?'

They hugged. 'Hiya. Just fine.'

'Hannah,' Emma drew her forward to meet a tall tanned man with raven curly hair and a tiny mirror image clinging to his knee. Daniel. 'This is my fiancé, Mal Webster.'

He stepped closer and shook her hand, smiling broadly. 'My pleasure Hannah. Heard all about you. Hope you're settling in.' He looked down fondly at the boy. 'This is my son, Daniel.'

Knowing strangers would be daunting to some children, she smiled warmly. 'Nice to meet you Daniel. You'll be looking forward to Noah getting here then?'

He grinned and nodded.

'Em, if you could put your bowl of salad through on the table and hand around those tempting savouries while they're still hot, I'll fix everyone a drink.'

The women chose wine, Mal poured himself a frothy beer but Will, Hannah noted, drank sparkling water. They raised their glasses and toasted friendship and Hannah's arrival.

'Are you missing family, Hannah?' Emma

asked gently, drawing her aside.

'At first but not now.' She amazed even herself by the statement. Her sisters and their problems so far away had filtered into the background of her thoughts since making new friends in Tingara. The charming village was slowly weaving its peaceful spell over her.

'Done much sightseeing?'

'I walk around town most days and Will lent me his charming old bicycle,' she teased, glancing across at him. They exchanged fond smiles and a knowing look passed between Emma and Mal.

To cover her embarrassment that she had allowed her feelings to be obvious, Hannah said, 'I rode out on one of the tourist trails to a cheese factory, a winery and a chocolate shop. Alma Powell's teaching me how to knit.'

'Well done.' Emma raised her eyebrows. 'Alma usually keeps to herself although our Will seems to have snuck under her radar. They're always swapping recipes but Will puts his own spin on them.'

The friends traded banter while Hannah stood back and watched the chirpy interplay among them. Soon Nick and his sons arrived with more introductions all around, and the noise level rose a few decibels as a result.

Hannah saw a big handsome man in jeans, cinched with a wide leather cowboy belt and checked shirt sleeves rolled up to the elbows, shadowed closely by three jostling boys. Daniel lit up at the sight of Noah and they disappeared into the sunroom to play. Tyler looked lost and moody, hands sunk into his hooded windcheater pockets, cap on backwards, reluctant to catch anyone's eye. Christopher settled on a sofa in the sunroom reading until dinner.

The father though, Hannah detected as she watched him during the early part of the evening, was a strong man outwardly holding it together but doing a good job of hiding strain and sadness beneath. It was clear there here was a good man's man who loved his sons, prompted easy gentle discipline when needed, his fatherly eye regularly flashing in his boys' direction at all times. Heartbreaking that he had been wronged by his wife.

Her own parents had provided a traditional and stable example and Hannah wanted nothing less than a lifetime commitment and love for herself.

'You okay?' Will whispered in her ear, suddenly beside her.

She smiled and nodded. 'Just reflecting.'

Then it was dinner and madness, laughter and chatter, and ferrying food platters into Will's magical dining space. He pulled out a chair for her next to him, everyone else seated themselves at random and a memorable night, for more than one reason, began.

Chapter 7

Throughout the meal it was so obvious that bubbly Emma and cheeky Mal glowed around each other. It tugged Hannah's heartstrings to see such a deep genuine warmth of love between them reflected in shared glances, smiles, touches and gestures of thoughtfulness and connection. With the pair both having previous unsatisfactory relationships, this time, it seemed, fate and the Gods of Romance had stepped in.

With Will right alongside her, Hannah's own emotions surged with tenderness for him so she was glad of the break between courses to give her wild imagination time to recover. She and Emma gathered up all the plates, the men refreshed drinks and Nick suggested Tyler and Christopher make themselves useful which meant everyone tripped over each other in the kitchen.

When all was organised for dessert and the gang seated around the table again, Will produced a huge apple cake with a crunchy topping of nuts and cinnamon sugar, and a large pottery jug.

Emma eyed it all with dismay. 'We're a bigger group tonight, Will. Five adults and four hungry boys. I guess its smaller slices, then?' she moaned.

Will shrugged. 'We have your fresh fruit platter, too. I'll bring it in.'

'Well at least tell us there's lashings of double cream in that jug and not low fat yoghurt,' she teased.

Everyone laughed. They all clicked so well that, just for a moment, Hannah felt like an outsider again. But they were such a friendly bunch of people, the brief tug of loneliness passed.

When Will disappeared into the kitchen again, long sad glances circled the table. He returned with a devilish grin and another cake of equal size to the first.

'Will Bennet. You beast.' Emma cried out, laughing. 'You're such a tease. Now *that's* more like it. Hannah,' she leaned forward across the table, 'this delectation will melt in your mouth. Don't skimp on a bite.'

Conversation effectively stalled as Will did the honours slicing, pouring and serving then everyone ate until there was only the sound of spoons scraping empty plates and deep sighs of satisfaction rolled around the table like a Mexican wave.

A lazy hum of dull conversation and

contentment became the mood until the boys nudged each other.

'Can we please be excused, Uncle Will?' Tyler asked, scowling.

'Sure, mate.'

'Bowls to the sink,' Nick reminded them.

An eager shuffle followed as the children all escaped.

'Sorry for the extra imposition tonight, mate,' Nick addressed Will. 'Couldn't get anyone to babysit.'

'It's fine, mate. They're good kids.'

'I don't need a babysitter,' Tyler growled from the kitchen, overhearing.

Nick shook his head and raised his voice. 'You don't but your brothers do.'

Will glanced at Hannah with raised eyebrows. She took his cue and said, 'Nick, I'm more than happy to help out while I'm here in the next two months. I have bags of free time.'

He dipped his head in embarrassment for a moment then raised a grateful gaze to meet hers. 'Thanks, Hannah. I might take you up on that.'

'I'll give you my mobile number before I leave.'

'Appreciate it.'

Will reached across in front of everyone and squeezed Hannah's hand. She was rattled to say the least at this show of affection from him among his closest friends. The simmering chemistry that had flared into life at their first meeting on St. Anne's front porch days after her arrival was now allowed rein. An exciting thought.

They fancied each other, for sure, but she knew deep in her heart she wanted this relationship to develop and be special. It felt…important. But how could they possibly pursue it from different countries? Crumbs. A long distance relationship? It couldn't possibly work. She would hate being apart.

Over Hannah's contemplations, Will said, 'No movement on the sale of that cottage next door to you, Nick?'

Since Will lacked a dishwasher, Emma and Mal offered to do the dishes. The four boys were playing happily in the sunroom, leaving just Will, Hannah and Nick lingering at the table.

'Actually, Anne Perry thinks she might have a buyer.'

'*Lakeside* must have been on the market for what, six months to a year now?'

Nick shrugged his broad admirable shoulders. 'A mud brick fixer-upper on acreage isn't for everyone. Take a special person I reckon.'

Nick was like a huge cuddly bear you just wanted to hug, Hannah thought. Any woman that teamed up with him would bag herself one real man. Complete with his deep voice and lazy sex appeal.

'Maybe your new neighbour will be a fetching

female,' Hannah teased, crossing her fingers for him.

'*Lakeside* would be too much hard work for a woman,' he drawled.

Dishes done, everyone retired to the deep comfy sofas in the sunroom, strung with fairy lights. Christopher already occupied one seat reading his book but vacated to sit happily cross legged on the floor, keeping his eyes on the page, scarcely missing a word as he moved.

'Good story?' Hannah asked in passing as the adults took seats, Nick in a single chair, Mal and Emma snuggled together on one sofa and Hannah settling into one end of another.

'Harry Potter.'

'Ah, that explains it.'

Will brought in a huge teapot and tray of pottery mugs with Hannah's box of chocolates. Subdued general conversation followed. Will huddled close to Hannah, shoulders and knees touching, making it obvious to her and everyone else in the room of his affection.

It wasn't late but Daniel soon crept onto Mal's knee looking sleepy.

'Looks like one young man needs bed soon.' He glanced at Emma.

She nodded. 'Any time.'

They left shortly after, Emma promising a girl's catch up with Hannah and swapping phone numbers. Then it was like a cascading fall of dominoes. First, Noah quietly sidled up to his father. The big man put his arm around the boy's shoulder and drew him close.

The touching love between parents and children seeped into the corners of Hannah's heart. She enjoyed children, loved babysitting her nephews back home in Oxford, reading bedtime stories. Checking on them while they slept until Heather and Michael returned from one of their regular nights out. Having no time or particular interest for a social life of her own, Hannah was inclined to feel like a maiden aunt instead of an older sister.

Next, Tyler sauntered in, lost, Chris trailing soon after.

Nick unwound himself from Noah, stretched and rose. 'Too easy to get comfortable. Come on, boys. Grab your coats and let's hit the road. Thanks for the evening, mate.' He shook hands with Will.

'Thank you for that box of goodies that I presume fell off the back of someone's truck?'

'Genuine seconds,' Nick chuckled. 'Enjoy. Lovely to meet you Hannah.'

'You, too.' She hesitated. 'Did you want my number? For the boys?' Tyler scowled. 'Just in case,' she said carefully.

They exchanged numbers and the all-male Logan tribe trooped out.

Left alone, Will and Hannah stared at each other. He didn't touch her but, crumbs, every part of her body was on high alert.

To break the ice more than anything, since Will remained disturbingly silent, she asked, 'Can I have a butcher's at the landscape painting you were working on?'

'Sure.'

He hesitated only a moment before strolling across the sunroom to a storage cupboard and produced it. He held it up from where he stood. At that distance, it placed his work into full landscape perspective.

Hannah gave a sigh of amazement. 'It's brilliant. I love it. You are seriously good, Will. Is it going in the exhibition?'

'Thanks.' He nodded, gave a sheepish grin and set it aside, sauntering back toward her again.

'How's it coming along? Your work for the exhibition.'

'Slowly.' He paused. 'I'm afraid to touch you,' he murmured.

Hannah laughed nervously at his confession and sudden switch in the conversation. 'Why should you be afraid of me?'

'You have no idea?' He sounded dubious as his heavy lazy gaze drifted all over her.

Speechless, she shook her head and tried to remember to breathe.

'Why do you think I keep my hands in my pockets around you?'

It wasn't a normal habit for him? Her mind blanked and she silently shrugged.

'I'm even afraid to be alone with you. I keep getting this blinding temptation to ravish you. I've wanted to push my hands up under that enticing soft jumper of yours all night and explore beneath.'

His words would be music to any woman's ears especially since she returned the feelings but what now?

'Cheeky,' she whispered as he stepped closer.

Ever so slowly, he leant into her and tasted her lips like an appetiser before a meal. 'Thanks for coming tonight and being thrown in the deep end with my friends.'

'They're all lively and fun.' Afraid of what might happen if she stayed, she said, 'Any road, I should head off now.'

'I'll walk you home.' He slid his feet into shoes and pulled on a coat before she could argue.

'Is that wise?' she teased, unsure what he expected.

'You don't need to invite me in but resist me if you dare,' came his husky taunt.

They held each other's freezing hands on the short brisk walk back to St. Anne's and had barely stepped up into the porch when he tugged her up against him, slid an arm tight around her waist and kissed her again. If the appetiser rocked her, the main course melted all resistance and left her weak at the knees. His body warmth flowed into hers and he smelt male and tempting.

They sought each other in a new and exploratory mutual hunger of discovery. Hannah's hands wandered up around his neck and into the long ends of his hair. Thick and silky soft, the strands slithered between her fingers and she sighed with pleasure. Was this man irresistible or what?

When they drew apart, both equally amazed and breathing raggedly, Hannah gently pressed her hands against Will's chest. 'Um, maybe step back and cool off?'

He laughed. 'Cool? It's bloody freezing out here. I need you to keep warm.'

'I think you have more in mind than that.'

'Damn. You're onto me already.'

He nibbled her mouth, setting off another episode of kissing.

Afterwards, he said, 'Looks like being a brief break in the weather next week. First mild day, are you still up for that *plein air* painting date?'

She might be bored stiff but she said, 'Absolutely.' She could always gawk at Will to pass the time.

'Bring a book or whatever.'

Great idea. Or her knitting project which was almost done.

As he gave her a final deep and lingering kiss goodnight, during which she seriously thought about inviting him inside, she wondered at the wisdom of encouraging her sexy neighbour but she fancied Will Bennett something wicked so even the thought of moderation and fighting her craving for the man was just plain barmy.

For once in her life, maybe she would just chuck being sensible.

After Will reluctantly left, Hannah reflected on the fallout of starting a more serious relationship with him and what happened when they had to part when she returned home to England?

She had lived a lonely stressful life before. Practically been a working robot. How had she endured? On holiday now she was practising cooking more, and knitting, and walking for miles, and had never felt better. Simple rewards in themselves. Why had she been foolish enough not to stop long enough to pursue these small pleasures back home?

Where at first she had feared boredom, in fact, in only a matter of weeks here in Tingara she had grown so involved in this small town community, met people, recognised friendly faces, had people wave to her in the street and on her long walks, that she almost felt like a local. Hard to remember her real home existed at all.

But it did and she must return to it. That old life. But not the same way she had lived before. Having glimpsed it, another way of life, experienced another place in the world, had opened her eyes to alternatives and opportunities. She would love to travel. Expand her horizons. Quite simply, live. Break away from the known and memories, and continue the change in herself which had already begun. Explore who she was and what she sought from life.

As Will predicted, a brief sunny string of days followed.

He trotted down to St. Anne's. 'Tomorrow?' he suggested after ravishing Hannah at the porch door before he had barely arrived.

Flustered by his breezy invasion and a foxy seduction, wondering where all this would lead, she nodded. He smelt fresh and looked dishy even in sloppy paint-splashed clothes.

'Just bring yourself. And food,' he murmured. He named a time and stole her lips again before he left.

Moving around St. Anne's, stunned for the rest of the day, Hannah knew purpose. She baked Alma's scones, packed her knitting and a book, and lay awake that night, adrenalin running through her veins with memories of how Will affected her every time she saw him. Hard to concentrate on a thing when he was around. Impossible to sleep.

Next morning, anticipation built as she awaited Will and impatiently paced St. Anne's, unwilling to stand on the street and wait, announcing the outing to the neighbourhood, especially Alma directly across the Lane who missed nothing.

So she waited indoors, and waited. Checked her watch and waited longer. Fifteen minutes late? She frowned. What had held him up? Maybe he'd had an accident or was ill? Should she go down to investigate? No. He would just tease her for fussing. At thirty minutes over and still no sign of him, Hannah left St. Anne's, locked it and left the picnic hamper under the porch.

All the way down the Lane to Will's place she imagined scary scenarios of what might have happened. His old car was backed out of its shed and parked in the driveway. A good sign. At least he was around and ready to go.

At the terrace French doors, she peered through the glass to see him frowning in concentration, apparently deeply focused and painting because he did not become aware of her. Hannah waited a moment then tapped on the glass, standing shivering in the chill despite the tepid warmth from the late morning sun.

He tossed her a blank stare of surprise then understanding dawned.

'Are you all right?' she asked as he opened the door.

'Sure. Why?'

She tapped her watch. 'You're late. It *is* today?'

'Of course,' he grinned, puzzled.

Honestly, that cute look on his face could get him out of any trouble. 'I was raised on the understanding that if you were going to be *this* late, you let the other party know. Out of courtesy,' she emphasised, annoyed that he wasn't in the least concerned at having kept her waiting.

Too swiftly for her to step away, he abruptly leaned forward and kissed her nose. 'I wasn't aware of the time so, technically, I didn't know I was late, did I?'

'Don't you check the time when you have an appointment?'

'Mostly.'

Hannah's irritation rose. 'That's inconsiderate.'

She wanted to be grumpy, show her frustration at his indifference to having upset and worried her. Unlike him.

'Did you have another commitment?' he asked.

'Of course not. I kept today free.'

'That's all right then.'

'All right for who? I don't appreciate being kept waiting and worrying for nothing. I would never do that to someone else unless it was unavoidable.'

'You worried?' Gentle regard softened his voice and gaze.

'Well of course I did. Anyone would.'

'Not everyone. That was sweet of you.'

'What were you doing?' She peered over his shoulder.

He half turned back to indicate the unfinished work on his easel. 'Trying to get the light perspective and blending accurate. That's why I wanted to get outdoors today while the sun's out.'

How annoying that the chap had a genuine reason for everything.

Refusing to be disarmed by the appreciation in his warm brown eyes, she backed away when he moved closer again. 'I'll be at St. Anne's.' She glanced over her shoulder. 'You can pick me up on the way past. When you're ready.'

'You're still coming?'

'Against my better judgement.'

His chuckle was infuriating as she closed the French door. Honestly, Will Bennett was such a wanker.

Another half hour passed during which Hannah reflected on artistic types and their apparent tendency to be vague. If Will was a typical example.

She heard him before she saw him. *Dora* roared down the Lane as though her driver needed to give it full throttle just to keep it going. A jaunty Will leapt from the vehicle in the driveway, beaming, apparently lucid again after his earlier creative fog and stowed Hannah's things into the small boot alongside his painting equipment and two deck chairs.

As she squeezed herself into the compact front seat, she was relieved to see seat belts and immediately clipped hers across. Still dogged by her fear of driving or riding in cars, a rush of panic rose up inside her with a feeling of being exposed in this flimsy old thing. It would be useless in an accident, wouldn't it? She practised deep breathing. Would this fear ever leave her? She hadn't driven since coming up anxiously to Tingara from the airport weeks ago.

'Is it safe?' she asked Will when he climbed in beside her and urged *Dora* into life.

Will glanced at her and frowned. 'I wouldn't take you otherwise and I certainly wouldn't be driving it myself. *Dora's* old and she has her moments but the garage keeps her running for me. Trust me,' he said gently, watching Hannah's angst. 'We can't go fast and I promise I'll be careful.' He took her hands between his own. 'What brought this on?'

'Nothing. Really.'

'I've never had a mishap but she has broken down once or twice.'

Hannah guessed, in his usual mischievous way, he was stretching the truth and smiled weakly. 'You've never thought to upgrade?'

'No need. She still goes and does everything I need around town. Usually.' He paused. 'Would it bother you to be stranded with me?'

'No,' she readily admitted, and meant it. They exchanged loaded glances.

They reversed from the driveway and headed up the Lane to the High Street, or Main Street as the locals here called it.

As they gathered speed on the road from town, she asked, 'How long have you had *Dora*?'

'Since I returned to Tingara about five years ago. Acquired it from an old timer who had lived here all his life and only driven it around town but couldn't drive anymore.'

'Can't have been worth much.'

'It was priceless to him. Meant independence into old age until his eyesight let him down. I didn't actually pay for it. It was a swap.'

'Really? What for?'

'One of my big local bush paintings which now hangs in his room in the aged care home. Ben saw it, suggested the deal and says it now reminds him of home. If he ever feels down he looks at it and imagines himself back in Tingara.'

Hannah felt suitably corrected. 'That's a lovely story.'

Will slowed to turn off the main sealed road and down a dirt bush track. It took a while but, as they drove, Hannah gradually relaxed, her former tension sliding away as *Dora* rattled along beneath Will's steady capable hands. Clearly, driver and vehicle knew each other's eccentricities.

The sun streamed over the green countryside and woodland, flickering between the sparse olive foliage of gum trees like countless diamond sparkles of light. This land was sombre in colour compared to the lush and vibrant emerald fields of home. Here, she had learned, they called them paddocks and when they crossed narrow bridges it wasn't over brooks or streams but, according to their named signs, it was creeks.

As *Dora* clattered and bounced along, Hannah trusted Will knew their destination. Suddenly he veered off the track and wound through the bush and trees. As they drew closer and their destination came into view, Hannah sighed over the idyllic scene. Worth the trip. An artist's secret paradise for sure. Postcard views by a rocky creek overhung by gums and willows, backed by the distant outlined curves of blue-hazed hills.

Will turned off the motor but made no move to leave the car. He hung his arms over the steering wheel as if entranced. 'This little pocket of nature never ceases to stun me every time I come back. I don't often visit. I like to keep it special.'

'It's lovely. A hidden gem for sure.'

'Every aspect and corner lends itself to a potential painting.'

They alighted together. While Will unpacked his gear, Hannah strolled to the sloping pebbly embankment. Crystal water, icy cold no doubt, rushed and slithered over and among smooth rocks. A light breeze tugged her hair, trembled leaves and brushed the tips of waving grasses.

'Could be a Constable, a Turner or Gainsborough country, couldn't it?' Will murmured coming up behind her.

'You have your own unique informal scenery here in Australia.'

He drew aside a heavy blonde fall of her hair and pressed his warm lips to the bare skin on her neck. A shiver of delight and longing scrolled through every inch of her body in response to his feather light touch. His hand rested at her waist and, standing silently together, they appreciated the beauty of this stunning winter day.

When Will moved away, Hannah felt deprived. He abandoned his art gear on the ground and began what she could only describe as a prowl. He stalked about, squinting and frowning, clearly seeking *the spot*.

Finally, he pointed to a gum tree overhanging the water. 'Over there.'

He strode back, retrieved his gear and moved. Hannah gathered her basket from *Dora's* boot and followed. Will was already setting up his French box easel, a paintbox with a lid on a tripod stand. He placed a canvas inside the raised lid and set out his palette of colours and brushes. From this angle, he would catch the bending gum tree against the watercolour blue wintry sky, the creek meandering through to one side and those misty hills beyond. His excitement was unmistakeable as he began, as though a fever had gripped him again like earlier back at his house.

Hannah understood silence might be wise so she chose a place for her chair nearby, backed up against the broad trunk of a huge ancient gum tree facing the sun and sheltered from even the lightest chill wind. Apart from sitting before her electric fire in St. Anne's, this was probably the warmest she had felt since arriving in Tingara.

Chapter 8

For a long while, engaged by her surroundings and the serenity of this secret place, Hannah did absolutely nothing. She stared up into the thin branches of the white flowering gum above, heaps of which she had already noticed about town, and watched screeching twittering birds so unlike those back home. Her book and knitting forgotten.

Will's voice echoed across the stillness and broke the hush. 'The big red and green birds are lorikeets and parrots. The pink and grey ones are galahs. And the tiny black and yellow ones darting everywhere are honeyeaters.

'How's it going?'

'I've covered the basics,' he murmured. 'Sky, earth and greens.'

'Can I see?'

'Not much on canvas at the moment.'

'Can I talk?'

He grinned. 'You already are.'

'Do you ever go down to the coast and paint the sea?'

'I did when I surfed and lived by the ocean.'

'How's your exhibition work coming along?'

'Under control. Have to head down to the city next week for an overnighter to see the gallery space and have a chat to the curator.'

She would miss him. 'It's getting closer. Excited?'

'Only if you come along. Want to see the big smoke and play tourist?'

Hannah's heart skipped and her mind raced. Would she be alone or with Will for all or part of the time, she wondered? She would love seeing Melbourne and spending time with Will but contemplated the overnight situation. No matter how much this chap thrilled her heart, it wasn't her style to be up for it after knowing someone for only a matter of weeks. Even with this lovable bedraggled artist. Maybe she was crossing bridges ahead of time.

'I'd love it.'

His face lit up with a broad smile. 'Ever been camping?'

Okay. Change of topic. 'In a tent? No.' Crumbs, where was this heading?

'Then you've been seriously deprived. We should go.'

There was a challenge. 'This time of year would be freezing. I would need to keep very warm.' She laughed at herself but caught Will's serious glance in return.

He stopped painting. 'That can be arranged.'

He eyed her with meaning. 'At night, you sit around a roaring campfire then snuggle down deep inside a feather sleeping bag.'

Hannah's mind ran riot again. It wasn't summer but a fan would cool her down nicely about now thank you. Two adventures to anticipate. With Will. Melbourne and camping. She hoped it was more like glamping. Tingara just kept getting better every single day.

As abruptly as it had begun, conversation lapsed and Will focused on painting again. Hannah actually became engrossed in her novel, a romantic suspense. At the end of a chapter, she closed her book and lazily stretched, turning aside to see how Will was going and caught him staring at her.

Embarrassed, she said quickly, 'Scones and hot tea yet?'

'Sure. Let's take a break.'

Hannah unpacked the hamper contents on the soft grass between their chairs, poured tea into their thermal mugs and produced a container of fresh scones, made to Alma's supposedly foolproof recipe. Not having made then before, Hannah could only hope. Half were spread with lashings of butter and sliced cheese, the remainder with raspberry jam compliments of Alma's pantry preserves.

She could be with this man forever, she just knew. For a while, they ate, drank and soaked up the view and atmosphere of this exceptional winter's day. But no matter how they both tried to ignore it, a suspense existed between them.

Finally, Will set down his mug and said roughly, 'I'm not looking forward to you leaving.'

Flattered, Hannah chuckled to make light of the moment and his words that sent a thrill to the deepest corners of her heart. 'I've only just arrived really. I still have two months.'

Her old life had been on hold. Then, suddenly, her parents' deaths, a random holiday decision and now this. Will.

'Not enough for me,' he growled, drawing closer, sliding an arm possessively across the front of her, pushing his fingers up underneath her thick hair and taking a long slow kiss.

He began warm and coaxing, gentle, seductive. Impossible for Hannah not to respond and get into it, so that their kiss deepened and their gathered tension was released into passion. Hannah's mug slipped from her fingers onto the grass. Her arms wound about his neck. Pressed tight against each other, they drifted into oblivion together.

Hannah knew only a resounding relief that Will felt the same way but that knowledge in itself created a niggling concern. She chose to ignore it, enjoy the moment, lost in his warmth and the exciting gentleness of his loving.

'Ah, Hannah Charles from England, you are *such* a distraction. How am I supposed to finish my exhibition on time with you around?'

'Should I stay away?'

He barked out a short ironic laugh. 'That won't help.' She was afraid to ask what would. 'Day or night I can't sleep or work for thinking of you.'

'Oh.' Bad for him, good for her? 'What should I do then?'

He chuckled. 'Stop looking so damned gorgeous and tempting.' He glanced at her and it seemed difficult for him when he admitted, 'I'm totally taken with you.'

'Thank you but let's not get ahead of ourselves, okay?'

'Smart *and* wise,' he whispered against her ear, lifting her hair, kissing her neck, giving her excited goose bumps all over.

With one finger he turned her face toward him. When he gave her that deep look, she knew she was desired and about to be kissed. Will Bennett was an open book. Honest, readable, adorable.

'You have the sweetest mouth,' he drawled and tasted her again.

Sunk into his arms, each craving more, the world receded and it was only the touch and feel and electricity with this man that held her attention. Nothing else mattered.

When they drew apart, he brushed the back of his hand across her cheek. With a reluctance she, too, fully understood, he rose and pulled

Hannah to her feet. He kissed her forehead, eyelids, nose, and a quick cheeky dip of her mouth, then sighed and snapped a glance back toward his easel.

'Think I'll call it quits. I have the basics down. I can finish it in the studio.'

'Sorry,' she murmured, not feeling in the least regretful.

'Don't be.' He grabbed her hand and tugged her to him. 'You are a truly lovely surprise in my life. When I was surfing, the girls chased *me*. Challenging to meet a woman who I respect on all levels for her beauty and independence and smarts.'

'Okay, I get it,' she laughed, embarrassed. 'You like me.'

'Hope the feeling's mutual?'

How could a man so magnetically attractive and oozing quiet charisma be so unsure of himself? 'Of course.'

They packed up and drove home in a silence humming with potential. At St. Anne's, Will carried her basket to the porch, kissed her goodbye and left.

Because Will sounded like he was struggling to complete his works for the exhibition, Hannah assumed she might not see him again until their planned trip to Melbourne. So it was a surprise when she opened the porch door to him the next day. His hair was damp and he held a comb and scissors in his hand.

'Hiya.'

'My hair needs a trim.' It did? How could he tell? She gaped and waited a moment, suspecting this might be a tease but he stayed serious. 'I need to look presentable for my promoter.'

Hannah thought he looked perfect but she was biased.

'Okay. I should warn you that I have absolutely no skills in this area.' Crumbs, where did she start?

He shrugged. 'Just a couple centimetres straight off the bottom length.'

'I'll see what I can do.' She stepped aside and gestured for him to enter.

'Women are the best hairdressers.'

'In your experience?'

He nodded. 'For my long hair I need a female touch. Most barbers only do short back and sides.'

'I like your style,' she admitted.

'You do?'

'Can't wait to get my hands on it.'

'A woman after my own heart,' he murmured, then sauntered the living areas glancing about. 'You're neat. Ginny would be stoked.'

'It wasn't a question she asked when we swapped. We were both keen to leave and loved each other's places.'

'So, are you feeling the benefit of this holiday?

Was it worth it?'

Loaded question. Was it ever. 'What with *plein air* sessions and meditation,' she joked, 'I'm practically stationary.' Will laughed. From deep in his chest. Hannah melted. 'So, how do we do this?'

'Need a small towel for around my neck. Ginny keeps them in a pile upstairs.' He nodded toward the mezzanine.

Either Ginny cut Will's hair or he was familiar with the woman's bedroom. Envy and indignation reared their ugly heads in Hannah's heart and mind but she squashed them for common sense. Of course he knew this church. He helped redesign it. Professionally, he would be familiar with every inch.

Ignorant of her confusion, Will pulled out a dining chair into the middle of the room and sat down.

After that, Hannah ran upstairs for the towel and returned, finding it rousing as she draped the towel, touching Will. His hair was thick and soft with natural blonde streaks lightening its natural sandy colour, and smelt of pine.

As she clipped it up and it flowed through her fingers while she trimmed, the stirring feelings and intimacy of her task, the dip of his suntanned neck beneath, the slight shadow of whiskers on his face that suggested he hadn't yet shaved today, warred with his comment about Ginny and hinted at a closer relationship between them than neighbours.

The quiet settled around then and neither spoke until she was done by which time Will's hair had almost dried and fell in natural waves touching his shoulders. Every woman who moaned about straight hair would be so envious.

As she stepped around in front of him to judge her efforts, Will stared at her intently. 'All done. I'll fetch a mirror and you can check its okay.'

He shook his head and stood up, casually pushing a hand through it in one fluid easy movement. He reminded her of a lithe muscled cheetah silently hunting prey.

'No need. I'm sure its fine.'

'When did you first grow it long?'

'Surfing days. It was the culture, the look.' He grinned. 'It drew chicks.'

'Lucky you.'

Did she wish she had known Will in his youth? He was a mature eyeful now. She could imagine how young female hearts had panted for him ten years ago, too. Will on a surfboard was a dynamic image. From the torso outlines beneath the snug tee shirts he occasionally wore, as opposed to his usual loose casual clothes, he possessed a toned body.

Will collected his comb and scissors and kissed her. 'I might have to try avoiding you for a few days. Need to set myself a schedule for a change, some deadlines and try to achieve them.

Focus on the exhibition,' he explained.

'Of course. Good luck.'

'Remind me never to accept any offer to have my own art show again.'

With a twinge, Hannah knew she wouldn't be here. Why had he even mentioned such an impossibility? Slip of the tongue? Wishful thinking? She smiled wistfully and, as quietly as Will had appeared, he left. Hannah watched him through the front arched windows as he strolled back down the Lane.

She wouldn't mope. She had something in mind to pursue and keep occupied. Vague thoughts of Victoria and Chelsea drifted into her mind. Hannah wasn't sure if it was a good or bad sign she hadn't heard anything from them all week and oddly, hadn't considered them much either. She could only presume or hope Vic had dumped her bully of a sugar daddy and Chelsea was preoccupied with her new boyfriend. Hannah knew the feeling.

Meeting Will Bennett was a piece of good fortune. He had entered her life to become a distraction in every way and to a far greater extent than she could possibly have imagined any chap could ever be, especially after their first regrettable meeting when she felt rubbish, he had brought her soup and she had only been rude in return. She cringed to remember.

After her usual long morning walk, Hannah settled to some serious research on Google starting with genealogy and people record websites which led her to one in particular that looked promising.

She registered to gain access to the records and began to hunt, finding online electoral rolls from decades past a gold mine of information. By a process of deduction, and with a purring Fluffy nestled on the sofa beside her, Hannah tapped away on her laptop for hours, completely absorbed, losing track of time. Excited to be closing in on a result.

She only stopped long enough to feed the cat and herself dinner before continuing until it grew late and her eyes stung from concentration. She paused and stretched, trotting up to the chancel kitchen to brew herself a cuppa. One discovery led to another and yet another. It was like the last few fast-paced chapters of a novel that raced towards a conclusion.

Finally, incredibly, Hannah knew success. She stared at the screen before her and couldn't believe her eyes. Her problem now was, despite all her efforts and what she had uncovered, would Alma even want to know.

Selfishly and, perhaps, unreasonably Hannah desperately wanted her informed, if only for closure. The poor woman must to a certain extent still be anchored in the past, not knowing, always wondering. And what about her sons? Would they care?

While Hannah wrestled with her dilemma,

too cowardly to approach Alma with her findings, the days slid by, her mind constantly flashing to thoughts of Will, missing his company yet knowing it was for a purpose. She hoped he achieved it.

As if by mutual instinct, Will contacted her the next day. In person. At St. Anne's. Leaning against the porch post. Judging by the weary unkempt look of him, he was using it to hold himself up and had probably managed little sleep. Nor had he bothered to change his paint-spotted clothes. At least he wasn't bare foot even if his feet were only covered in his old plastic slip on gardening Crocs. He slid them off.

'Hiya,' Hannah greeted softly. She dared not speak loud for fear of disturbing his fatigue. 'Have you been standing 24/7 since I saw you last?'

'Guilty. But that wasn't the hard part. It's been very difficult avoiding you.'

He grinned, kissed her with warm abandon in greeting and moved past her to collapse on a sofa inside. 'I'm knackered.' He ran a hand across his face.

'I'd offer you something stronger than tea in the hope of revival but you don't drink, do you?' She tucked a leg beneath her and sat alongside.

'I make the occasional exception.'

'Do you have a reason to celebrate? Like finishing your exhibition?' she ventured.

He raised a hand and they high fived.

'Well done,' Hannah laughed.

'Did you miss me?' he drawled.

Should she be honest? She wrinkled her nose. 'A bit.'

'Ouch! I was hoping for *heaps* or *desperately*. Bit of a blow to my ego there.'

'It *was* lonely at times,' she admitted, 'but I kept myself occupied.'

She itched to tell him what she found but Will was in no condition to deal with what she feared might become a contentious issue between them. Maybe after he'd had a good sleep.

'We get to spend time together again in the coming days. Is tomorrow too soon for the Melbourne trip?'

She shook her head. 'Whenever you need to go.'

'I phoned the gallery. Perry wants to see a couple sample works as soon as possible and photos of the rest. I'll put it all together today. XPT train from Albury leaves mid-afternoon. I'll swing by after lunch. I'll book first class but I may need to sleep,' he warned.

'Brilliant. I'm looking forward to seeing Melbourne.' She hesitated. 'I'll understand if you're busy. I can sightsee on my own. I'll find my way around.'

He assessed her steadily for a moment with a gaze that bordered on seductive possession. In that moment, Hannah almost felt like she belonged to him. But not quite yet. There was one more step to take. And, quite frankly, she longed for it.

'It will be my pleasure to show you around. If you don't mind spending a while at the gallery with me first?'

'I'd love it.' She thrilled to know they would be mostly together and that Will wanted her with him.

'Bring comfortable shoes. We'll be doing lots of walking,' he suggested as he slowly rose.

He was leaving already? Hannah felt robbed. But he drew her up, too, crushed her against him and kissed her thoroughly again. A lovely reward for her patience.

It troubled her though that this friendship was becoming so much more than she could ever have imagined possible. Tingara was supposed to be nothing more than a holiday, a regrouping of her life and emotions, when it had evolved to become a potentially important romance with a chap she would not have ordinarily given a second look.

At another time and in other circumstances, Will Bennett may not have appealed. He was everything David was not but exactly what she was drawn to and needed. Hannah sensed it from their first meeting.

'Hannah?' Will was staring at her.

'Sorry?'

'Tomorrow then?'

'Absolutely.'

She walked him out, he took the liberty of more kisses on the porch, slid his bare feet back into his shoes and left.

Hannah ducked over to Alma, bursting to reveal her discovery but instead asked if she could feed Fluffy while she was away.

'Of course, dear. I'll do it same time as I do Callie for Will. You have yourselves a nice time in the city.'

'Thanks.' Hannah gave a quick smile, wondering if Alma thought she and Will were sleeping together. She wished. It hadn't progressed quite that far. Yet. But it did raise the question of who else was speculating in town. Were they the subject of gossip? The locals did love to share any titbit of news.

Next afternoon, Hannah's stomach curled with desire at the sight of Will. His sandy wavy hair, freshly trimmed by yours truly, brushed his white shirt collar. What a transformation! Her heart fluttered. His jeans fitted tight and a tailored sports coat – she recognised quality when she saw it, man and clothes – draped casually open. One yummy artist.

His gaze as he emerged from *Dora* reflected her own ache of longing. She wore a long knit tunic over leggings and boots with a pair of Emma's beautiful chandelier earrings swinging and glinting from her lobes.

'Hi gorgeous,' he whispered in greeting.

She chuckled. 'Charmer. You've scrubbed up

yourself.' She eyed him hungrily up and down, not normally this bold with men, but around Will she felt safe and comfortable. What would be, would be. Without pressure.

Crumbs, she would need to rein herself in or they would end up in bed together. Which she desperately wanted. At the right time. She wasn't even sure she was ready for the next step. If she could handle an affair with Will then leave him to return to her own life in another country.

As wild fantasies played out in her mind, Will stowed her small overnight bag in the boot and they were off. Within half an hour they arrived in Albury and parked at the station. Hannah followed him into the grand old ornate red and cream brick building with its impressive clock tower. Ornate metal columns ran like an avenue down either side of the long covered platform.

On the train, Will lifted their bags overhead plus three of his carefully wrapped smaller paintings and settled into the comfortable recliner seats.

When they were underway and speeding through the winter green countryside, Hannah innocently asked, 'Are you intending to catch up with your family in Melbourne?' The instant he flashed her a dark look, she realised her mistake and cringed.

'If you mean my parents that would be pushing the love too far. They won't be interested anyway. My painting has always been a sticky point for them. *Architect* sounds more impressive than *struggling artist,*' he said with a cynical twist of his mouth.

'Your brother and sister?'

Will shook his head and sighed. 'Hannah, stop making me feel guilty.'

'It wasn't my intention,' she protested. 'You said you keep in touch with them.'

'I do.'

'Doesn't sound like it.'

'Don't be pushy.'

'Where do they live? Close to the city or further out?'

Will scowled and gave a careless shrug. 'Close actually,' he seemed reluctant to admit. 'Courtney is in Albert Park and Lew is an inner city boy and hipster living in trendy Brunswick.'

'So?' Hannah nudged him, grinning.

Will scoffed. 'All right. I'll phone them and see if we can meet.'

Family was important to Hannah and she longed for more of it for Will so she pushed a little further. 'Do they even know about your first major solo exhibition?'

He grimaced. 'I'll tell them if and when we meet up, okay?'

'Have they seen your fabulous work?' He nodded. 'That's something.'

Will studied her for a moment before he said darkly, 'Not everyone gets to play happy families.'

After that, Hannah decided she best pull back and abandoned any further conversation, keeping silent. She absorbed the scenery while it was still daylight. Lulled by the train's gentle movement, she dozed. When she woke, Will was asleep. She watched him until darkness fell and city lights came into view.

Will stirred, the train pulled into the station and they disembarked to the noise and city bustle, highlighting the peace of Tingara and her country holiday.

A taxi brought them to a small artsy boutique hotel where they checked into separate adjoining rooms.

At their doors, Will said, 'Half an hour and we can eat in the bistro downstairs, okay?'

Hannah nodded.

Over dinner and subdued but easy chat, Will said, 'I phoned my sibs. We can all meet for coffee or an early light dinner tomorrow before our evening train.'

'Grand.'

'A restaurant on Southbank on the river?'

'Sounds lovely.'

'Only time to squeeze it in, I'm afraid. We'll be all morning at the gallery I expect and then I want you to myself in the afternoon for sightseeing before the sibs descend later.'

'My personal tour guide?' Hannah thrilled that he wanted that time alone together.

'Nothing less.'

They rode the lift back up to their rooms, Will's arm draped lovingly about her shoulder, although Hannah noticed he leant back against the wall with his eyes closed.

At their rooms, Hannah said, 'You're exhausted. Get a good sleep.'

His lips sought hers, warm and tender, loaded with promise. She sank against him, arms about his neck, his hands caressing her body, making it sing.

'Soon?' he whispered.

Hannah nodded and smiled. 'Promise. But not tonight,' she chuckled.

As she undressed and climbed into bed, she hugged their growing intimacy greedily to herself.

Chapter 9

Next thing Hannah knew was the sound of loud knocking on her door. Pushing herself drowsily from bed and pulling on a hotel robe, she padded barefoot to the door.

Will stood outside, beaming, looking the better for sleep, behind a laden breakfast trolley.

'Took the liberty,' he bowled past her and into the room, crossing to the windows to draw the heavy drapes.

She inhaled deeply. 'Fresh coffee. And a pot of tea.' She lifted the lids. 'Pancakes. Eggs. Toast. Fruit. Cereal. You're a marvel.'

Hannah was about to indulge when he caught her hand. 'No good morning kiss for the waiter?' he drawled.

She laughed and managed a quick peck on the cheek.

He pouted. 'Disappointing.'

'I'm hungry,' she protested.

'Clearly for food, not me. I'll claim the interest on my personal service later.'

They ate amid lively banter. As they both sat

drinking tea, Hannah asked, 'What time do we leave?'

Will shrugged. 'Appointment's at ten. Leave fifteen before? Gallery's close but we'll need a taxi with my paintings to deliver.'

'Brilliant. No rush then. I'll have time to shower and make myself presentable.'

'Hannah, you look adorable in PJs,' he murmured, sending her a suggestive glance. 'Pity I can't stay. Need to go write up descriptions for each piece I brought down.' When he stretched, she just wanted to stand up and wrap her arms around him. 'Too tired on the train yesterday and after dinner last night.'

'I noticed. You're much brighter this morning.'

He winked. 'I'm frisky so watch out.'

She laughed, shooed him out the door and they caught up again later.

A short taxi ride with Will carrying a handled bag of his paintings brought them to the gallery on a corner site of an inner suburb. Surrounded by narrow renovated terrace homes and an eclectic mix of shops and cafes, the precinct of lanes and small streets oozed an urban village charm.

Gallery owner, Perry, with his shaved head, sleek suit and pointy shoes was gushy and professional. It was immediately clear he knew his business and that Will's exhibition was in safe hands. The compact gleaming white space and plain walls looked larger, thanks to skylights, large paned front windows directly overlooking the street and targeted track lighting.

Hannah felt Will's enthusiasm hum. After introductions all round, he unpacked his paintings and Perry raved. Hannah stepped aside and listened for a while as they discussed pricing, flyers, advertising and how each piece should best be presented. All fascinating. Perry had everything in hand including the catering for opening night champers, wine and finger foods.

Seeing their deep absorption, Hannah indicated and mouthed to Will as she left, deciding to stroll in the local if chilly windswept streets.

'Won't be long,' she murmured.

He smiled and gave a thumbs up. He found her later in an artsy gift shop.

'Ready for lunch?'

'I'm still recovering from breakfast but why not?' she laughed, happy to see him again.

They held hands and strolled, finding a cosy café.

'All sorted?' she asked as they tucked into beef pot pies.

'Perry's a genius. He loved my work, is onto it, so I just need to pack up the rest of my canvases to be trucked down by his own guy especially employed for the purpose.'

'Getting excited?'

'The pricing he suggested scared me stiff. Not sure people will pay the dollars but he was adamant.'

'I envy and admire your talent. Knitting a garter stitch scarf is the extent of my art and crafty abilities.'

'I'm sure you have others,' he murmured suggestively, grinning. 'Plus you're a qualified professional.'

Then he dragged her away into another taxi that took them over the river to the Royal Botanic gardens. Rugged up, they linked arms and sauntered by lakes and ponds, appreciating the camellia gardens in full bloom.

Later, they hopped a tram out to St. Kilda on the beach and braved a cutting breeze off the water to walk the one kilometre pier to a kiosk at the end where they warmed up with marshmallow-loaded hot chocolates.

Freezing and laughing, they almost ran back, arms around each other. For warmth, Will claimed.

As they jumped down from the tram on the return trip and strode out along Southbank to meet Courtney and Lewis, Hannah wondered what they would read into her friendship with their brother. Honestly, she wasn't sure herself. Except that just simply being with him, watching him smile, seeing the wind ruffle that sexy long hair and be the beneficiary of his warm gazes, lifted her heart. Just slightly daunting that they lived so far apart.

Strolling the river's promenade with views across the water to the city, Hannah found it hard to focus and appreciate the arresting panorama, distracted by Will's stirring company and the prospect of shortly meeting some of his family.

As they approached a Spanish tapas bar, Will released Hannah's hand when his attention drifted to a man and woman already seated in a booth. He returned their wave. Inside was rustic with exposed brick walls and a cosy informal atmosphere. And way warmer than outdoors.

Hannah quickly combed fingers through her long tangled hair in an attempt to tame and tidy it after being windblown down on the bay.

Brother and sister rose to greet them. The brothers did the manly hug thing and Will air-kissed his sister on the cheek. He turned aside to Hannah and drew her close, an arm about her waist. She noted the siblings' interest rise at his gesture.

'This is Hannah Charles from England. My brother Lewis and sister Courtney.'

No pretensions here, Hannah observed. They all hugged and kissed, so she relaxed. The siblings' likeness to each other was distinct. Flaxen hair and broad cheeky smiles. For all Will's revelation about the pressured home in which he had been raised, these three adults appeared to have survived.

Lewis with his dyed white-blonde hair, shaved at the sides and lightly spiked on top. His clothes stylish. The kind of chap you could confidently ask for fashion advice. Courtney quietly sparkled. Softly draped in a maxi dress with leggings beneath and ankle boots. Feminine but trendy. With her styled long wavy hair floating about her shoulders and perfect makeup, Hannah felt dowdy.

'You managed to get away then?' Will addressed Courtney.

'You know Charlotte has a nanny, you tease.'

'Of course,' Will said dryly.

'Don't start,' she cautioned, grinning. 'I love my yuppie city lifestyle. It isn't wrong simply because you disagree.'

'As long as you're happy.'

'Reasonably.'

'Let me know if that ever changes.'

'Yes, big brother.'

Amid their gentle ribbing, Hannah glimpsed Will from another perspective. That of devoted and protective older brother.

'Everything right with you, mate?' he asked Lewis.

His brother pouted. 'Henry is in Sydney all week.'

Hannah guessed this was probably his partner.

'So,' Lewis turned a devilish gaze on her,

'how did you two meet?'

Courtney leaned forward. 'We only ask because with our big brother being buried in Tingara, it's a rare treat to even see him in the city, let alone with a *friend,*' she enunciated carefully.

Hannah glanced at Will and he gestured that she should explain.

'I'm here on a three month house swap actually. In St. Anne's on Gum Tree Lane.'

'Ah, so you're neighbours.'

'Temporarily.'

'Handy,' Courtney smiled. 'Isn't that the church you helped redesign for that business woman, William?'

He nodded.

'It's a beautiful and unique transformation,' Hannah said. 'I love staying there.'

'You don't feel isolated in a small country town?' Courtney asked.

'I've lived in a village back home all my life but I work in Oxford.'

They ordered sharing plates of hot nibbles, and drinks. Conversation flowed easily during which Hannah learned Courtney was a closet fashion designer and Lewis an IT guru with a raw and brash sense of humour. Confronting but honest. He and Will could not be more different. One the obvious extrovert yet all three bound by the bond of family.

Checking his watch, Will glanced

apologetically at his siblings then said to Hannah, 'We should go. Our train leaves soon.'

At least he was punctual for public transport, if not a *plein air* session, Hannah thought wryly as everyone rose, hugged and said goodbyes, promising to catch up at Will's exhibition in a few weeks.

Being in the dark, the return train journey was less interesting than travelling down the day before but Will, stimulated by the visit, said, 'Perry wants me to do a couple more smaller works if I can manage it in time,' he sighed, reaching for Hannah's hand. 'Might not see much of you again in the meantime.'

He discussed his ideas for possible new paintings, his adrenalin still pulsing. Because he was in such a positive mood, Hannah reflected whether now might be a good time to confide what nagged her mind. He should be more receptive and she really wanted to run it by him before speaking to Alma about it.

Whilst weighing up her options, she must have grown serious for Will asked suddenly, 'You okay?'

'Yes. Why?'

'You're sighing heavily.'

She closed her eyes and blurted out, 'I've done something you won't like.' No going back now.

'How do you know-?'

'I did some research. Alma's husband, Bernie,

is dead.'

He snapped a sharp glance at her. 'Did she ask you to find out?'

She knew he would ask her that. Here it comes, Hannah thought. The objections, the condemnation. She shook her head.

'Bloody hell, Hannah.'

She reeled back. Will never swore. He wasn't that sort of coarse chap. He pushed a hand roughly through his hair.

'I only wanted to help her,' Hannah said mildly.

'You should back off. It's not your place. Interfering in families.'

Did he mean his own as well, she wondered? 'Deep down I feel Alma would want to know. She certainly deserves to not have that great unknown hanging over her anymore.'

'Don't interfere. You'll stir up dust.' He turned to her, scowling. 'You can't always fix everything, you know.'

'What do you mean?'

'You can't stop yourself, can you? Deep down you probably mean well but have you ever stopped to think why you do this stuff? Sounds like you're on call for your sisters organising their lives.'

'*They* ask *me*,' she objected in her own defence.

'If you say so.'

Hannah flinched, offended that he would

doubt her word.

'You tried to get me together with my parents, who you should know haven't bothered to contact me for years and wrote me off as a teenager. And now you want to be the Holy Grail for Alma.'

Hannah fell silent, shocked by a usually complacent Will's outraged reaction, and stunned by his criticism. Given cause to reflect if she actually *did* interfere in people's lives. She always believed she was just trying to help.

She glared out the train window into the dark, seeing only her own miserable reflection back. Bollocks. She should have kept her mouth shut. Surely even Will himself and long-time Tingara residents must have all wondered over the years what happened to Bernie Powell? The night Hannah had dinner at Alma's house, she sensed that either from a lack of support in her search or knowledge on how to proceed, Alma wanted to know. She had brushed Hannah's query aside too quickly, claiming she didn't care. Between women, she suspected Alma had lied, perhaps wanting to know the truth but afraid of what she might discover.

And Will hadn't even reined in his anger long enough to care and ask what had happened to Alma's husband, missing by her calculations for over thirty years.

If this had happened to Hannah herself, she honestly would want to know. For peace of mind alone. To stop wondering, fearing even.

Sick with regret at having said anything to Will, getting stony silence and bad vibes from him seated beside her, Hannah closed her eyes and forced herself to doze, waking from her exhausted strain only when they reached Albury station.

No chance of more naps as they rattled back to Tingara in *Dora* in the middle of the night, the taut silence between them crackling. At this hour, Hannah didn't care. Maybe she would tomorrow.

Will stopped on the street in front of St. Anne's. Good manners ensured he lifted her case from the boot but he stood back in the dark, legs apart, hands on hips. No kisses tonight. Nor did she want any.

'Thank you for inviting me to Melbourne,' she said with soft weariness. 'I enjoyed seeing the city and meeting Courtney and Lewis.' She yanked up her trolley handle and headed down the driveway pulling it behind her. 'See you around,' she said carelessly over her shoulder. 'Or not,' she muttered to herself as she reached the porch.

Fluffy mewed at her feet and she bent to stroke her. At least someone was pleased to see her. If Will Bennett wanted her company he could ruddy well ask.

Tossing and turning during the night, Hannah decided maybe she and Will weren't that compatible after all. True, she felt a need to help people in distress or loss. Especially Will, although his family situation was probably futile which saddened her immensely on his behalf. Then she pulled herself up for having any sympathy for him. When it came right down to it, your family was the core of life. Who wouldn't want that?

As for her reliant sisters – possibly her fault, she conceded – for willingly taking on their troubles. Will had asked why? The niggling reality still lay with her own feelings of guilt over her parents' deaths. She probably could have had counselling. Talked to someone, anyone, but pushed opportunities away and lost herself in work.

Well, Tingara had her on the road to recovery. The scariest thing was having to face it all and make changes when she returned home. But feeling rested, calmer, practising yoga and meditation most days, the lovely long walks she so enjoyed around town, had eased her soul. It was bringing her peace. She acknowledged her lack but was working through things and dealing with them. She had made friends and would ensure she did again when she returned home.

She promised herself her life and work would slow down. She might even use up her leave, just take off and travel. Find more of her true self. Couldn't hurt. As all these thoughts scrolled through her mind, Hannah refused to think about Tingara and what she would leave behind.

Over the following days, Hannah clung to her knowledge of Bernie Powell and knew the worst angst over whether to trot across the Lane and visit Alma or not.

One morning, she simply sat up in bed, a coffee in hand, Fluffy purring at her feet. Indulging herself as she had grown blissfully accustomed on these gloomy wintry Tingara days when the sun refused to shine, knowing a greater peace than she had in a long time. Because there were no memories here and therefore solace, less interruption from her sisters. Her life was falling into place.

When her mobile buzzed with a Facetime call, she presumed it would be Chelsea. Absently, she pressed the button but, instead of her youngest sister, Ginny Bates appeared.

'Hiya,' she greeted her in surprise.

Crumbs, the woman was perfectly groomed, red nails, talked with her hands and plunged right in to the reason for her call. Hannah cringed. Was she about to blast her over Chelsea's monster phone bill?

'Your sisters have been appearing at the cottage on weekends. Acting like they own the place, intruding on my life. I gave them a short shove, told them not to bother me. I am entitled to my privacy and space while I'm here. Just to let you know in case they contact you and complain.'

Hannah smiled to herself. Seems like Ginny had everything under control her end. Her sisters had been told.

Before she could respond, Ginny added, 'Honestly, Hannah, how do you put up with those girls?'

'They *are* demanding.'

'Bloody selfish and useless, and I told them so.'

Hannah's body washed hot and cold. She stifled a chuckle. That wouldn't have gone down too well. 'You did?' She had often longed to do exactly the same.

'Absolutely. So, how is my house?' Again, Hannah opened her mouth to speak but Ginny went on with, 'I suppose you've discovered Will the charmer? Makes you feel like you're the only person in the world? Always doing small things for you? Am I right?'

Hannah hated to have her glowing bubble of approval for Will burst by Ginny's harsh unkind laugh. 'Yes, he's very thoughtful.' She played it cool. He wasn't her favourite person right now but she would defend his good character to anyone.

'He's quite a trophy for a woman. We were an item once, you know.'

Hannah stung to hear the admission. Ginny and Will? Totally hard to believe. 'Really?'

'I know what you're thinking. Impossible,

huh? Unlikely even. But it worked because I only occasionally came up to Tingara. No chance for boredom, if you know what I mean,' her voice lowered and she chuckled again.

'I'm surprised you wanted to be separate from him for so long then,' Hannah put in cheekily.

Hannah imagined the head thrown back to accompany Ginny's harsh laugh. 'God, no. Will's fun for a while but he has absolutely no ambition, honey.'

Hannah thought otherwise and took offence on his behalf. 'I've seen his work. He's a talented artist.'

'His little paintings and murals? Boys' stuff. Can't see he'll ever make a decent living from *that.*'

Well from what Will had told her, he already was and he was also an architect and property developer. Hannah had never heard such unreasoned detraction. She itched to boast about his upcoming debut Melbourne exhibition but she suspected Ginny would only denigrate the accomplishment and Hannah refused to give her that satisfaction. But she nonetheless bristled with indignation that anyone would be so critical and unkind of the harmless Will she knew, despite being estranged right now.

'No,' Ginny continued, 'Will Bennett is your classic small town nobody. But I knew that when I jumped into bed with him. I never intended it to last.'

They had slept together? Hannah was speechless but it didn't matter because Ginny happily chatted on.

'Hannah honey, a word of warning. Don't be sucked in by that long hair and cute backside. Every woman is turned on by the bad boy hippie. That air of mystery and danger about him. A man who shuns the system and is so enticingly different. I loved it, too. For a while. I can see why you would be attracted but you're a clever girl, I'm sure. You won't fall for his trap. Of course I wasn't fooled. My eyes were wide open. Well, I must dash,' she rambled on. 'I have to say, apart from your sisters turning up rudely and unannounced, the cottage is adorable. I just love it. It's entirely sweet but the two hour commute by train from here into London just isn't working for me. I'll be asking the company for a private helicopter.'

Good luck, Hannah thought. Where was *that* going to land in Snowshill?

Ginny had already ended the call. Hannah tossed the phone away across the bed. Ginny and Will? The woman sure knew him well, had sketched his exact personality and given more information than she cared to know. Or did she?

Images of them sleeping together crowded her mind. God, in this bed? Hannah wondered. She tried to get her head around Will with other women. There had been the surfie chicks in his youth but in recent times? Alma hadn't mentioned any and even Courtney said it was rare to see him with a *friend*, as she put it. Just because there hadn't been one in his life when she arrived, would he forget her and take up with Ginny again after she left?

Hannah shook her head. He couldn't possibly have faked all those kisses and admission of feelings and loving words. And not mean them. It just wasn't … Will.

All the same, the seed was sown and Hannah knew she might need to shelve her feelings. Play cool. Push him into the back of her mind – yeah, right – and keep busy. It worked for grief. Maybe it would help a reckless holiday romance, too.

She knew exactly what she wanted to do. Had done for days now but was plagued by doubt and deserted by courage. She argued with herself, dithered, but eventually caved.

Will wouldn't agree with what she was about to do but he needn't know. And even if he did, right now, feeling so confused about him as she did, Hannah really didn't care. Deep down, despite misgivings, Hannah still believed this was the right course of action.

At least Alma would know.

Chapter 10

Next morning after breakfast, without giving herself time to think, Hannah packed up her iPad notes to stride far less confidently than she felt, across the Lane to Alma's cottage.

'What a lovely surprise, dear.'

'Do you have a minute? Something I'd like to show you.'

'Of course, dear. Always for you.'

Hannah wasn't quite so convinced she would be welcome under Alma's roof again but she trusted her instincts. They made small chit chat in the kitchen already filled with wonderful baking aromas while Alma brewed a pot of tea.

'Should we pop into the sitting room?' Hannah suggested. What she intended to share might take time so they might as well be comfortable.

Alma carried the tray through, poured and settled back on the sofa beside Hannah.

'Now, what do you have there?' she indicated Hannah's papers.

'Please don't be cross with me but I've been

presumptuous and done some research.' She glanced across at the wedding photo of Bernie and Alma on the mantel. 'I know I didn't ask your permission but I couldn't bear the thought of you never knowing what happened to your husband.'

Alma's cup clattered unsteadily back into its saucer as her hand shook and she placed it on the tray. Then she straightened, her back rigid, hands folded in her lap and drilled Hannah with a forbidding stare. But not, she sensed, from outrage. The expression on Alma's face was certainly shock but also suspicion and dread.

Understandably she was afraid of what Hannah might tell her.

Hannah reached out a hand and laid it over hers, crossed so tightly into a fist. 'Bernie's dead, Alma,' she said gently.

Instantly, her shoulders drooped. She closed her eyes for a moment and began to tremble.

'Are you all right?'

Alma opened her eyes and nodded but Hannah didn't believe her for a second. Her lips quivered and she scrambled for a handkerchief in her apron pocket.

'Alma, I'm so sorry. After all this time, I know it will be a shock.'

Tears rolled down Alma's lined cheeks and Hannah felt helpless, knowing she was responsible for the upset.

'You don't feel faint or anything?' Alma

shook her head furiously. 'Should I fetch some sherry?'

Alma blew her nose, sniffed and said, 'I'm fine, dear, really.' She released a long slow sigh. 'Don't tell a soul I said this, dear, but you have no idea what a relief it is to know. One way or the other. I won't have to look over my shoulder any more, feel as if I'm being watched, afraid he might turn up again. He was awful violent when he was drunk.

'After he first disappeared, I was terrified he would return. I just wanted to be left alone with my little boys. My knees were raw from kneeling and praying that I never saw him again.'

Hannah was more than slightly relieved at what she was hearing. 'Will thought you wouldn't want to know.'

'Oh.' Alma waved an arm. 'Men aren't always right, dear.' She leaned forward. 'No matter how kind hearted and charming they are.'

Hannah blushed at the twinkle in Alma's moist eyes. She meant Will of course.

'Well, tea simply won't do. Fetch me that second bottle of wine you brought me from the pantry. Glasses are in the sideboard.'

When she returned, Alma toasted, 'To you, dear,' catching Hannah by surprise. 'For having the insight and thoughtfulness to do this for me. And my sons. Being younger, Tony and Sam really don't remember their father much. Probably for the best. But, as the oldest, Martin does. He'll want to know.'

Hannah waited. There was no rush, and gave Alma time to gather her thoughts. After one glass of rosé and a top up with a second, nibbling on still warm freshly homemade crispy sugar biscuits, Alma appeared more composed.

Wringing the damp handkerchief in her hands, she said, 'Perhaps you could tell me what you found now, dear.'

Hannah settled back onto the sofa, from time to time consulting her notes.

'I checked the old voters' rolls first and it seems he virtually went straight up to the outback opal fields of western Queensland. Cunnamulla.'

'He returned to where he was born!' Alma whispered in amazement.

'And that's where he prospected for opals ever since. He died less than a year ago and is buried there, too.' She handed Alma a piece of paper. 'These are the details. You might want to obtain a death certificate.'

'Oh, I'm not sure it's necessary and I'll bother, dear. It's enough to know.'

'The thing is,' Hannah continued, 'you might find you need one.'

Alma gazed at her blankly. 'What on earth for?'

'I phoned the district historical society up there, to see what else I could find. They put me onto a man who was born in Cunnamulla and still lives there. Old George. He was a prospecting mate of your husband apparently. I lied and said I was phoning on your behalf, explained your family situation and could he help me with any further details or information about Bernie. He was shocked to hear he married. Everyone believed him an old single bachelor. Then he was bluntly honest with me. Do you want to hear what he said?'

'Of course.'

'George said Bernie should never have married. Said he was surprised he lasted in civilisation with you as long as he did. And he was even more surprised to hear he had three sons. Said Bernie was born to be a loner. And get this. George said he never drank! Not sure I believe that or not but he loved the bush and was content.'

'Oh dear.'

'If it's any consolation, George said you really must have taken his heart for him to settle down for so long. But he never would have expected you to live in such harsh conditions in the outback.'

'So,' Alma said slowly, 'He just couldn't stand it anymore and left?'

Hannah nodded. 'Sounds like it, doesn't it?'

'And the drinking covered his unhappiness. If only he'd said.'

'He...left a safety deposit box at the Cunnamulla bank. They still hold it. As next of kin, you're entitled to whatever it contains. That's why, if you intend to investigate, you would potentially need a death certificate,' Hannah suggested.

'I can't do anything about that from down here. Cunnamulla's at the top of Australia.'

Hannah grinned. 'Pretty much. Perhaps when you explain it to Martin he can investigate for you.'

'We'll see,' Alma said cautiously. 'It's a long way and the young ones are always so busy these days.'

Hannah could only think regretfully to herself what a wonderful humble mother Alma's sons were missing in their lives. If it had been simple enough for Hannah to find out the information about their father, it would have been equally easy for any one of them to do the same. For their mother's sake if not their own.

After Hannah asked Alma one last thing, the older woman was in reasonably high and positive spirits when she left her, and not just from the wine. She talked of actually telephoning her son, Martin, but Hannah also knew without doubt Alma was also relieved and grateful to finally know what had happened to her missing husband after all these years.

Walking back across the Lane to St. Anne's, Hannah knew a personal sense of satisfaction and vindication to have ignored Will's warning and gone with her hunch in the matter. But then, she was all about family, Will less so.

The week dragged with no sign of Will although Hannah noticed one icy morning as she went for her walk that a large white van was parked in the Lane outside his house. From the gallery in Melbourne probably, collecting his works for the exhibition.

She missed him. Ached with longing to see him, talk, be kissed and feel loved as she never had before. Her holiday in Tingara was half over. She would be devastated without his company if he didn't want her for the rest of her stay.

She had already decided, whether he invited her or not, she would still attend his exhibition alone. She could always swallow her pride, suck up her exasperation with him and go visit Will but he made it clear he needed to focus on those last paintings Perry requested for the show. Pity, she sighed. She would love to gatecrash. So, with great difficulty, but respect for his privacy, she stayed away.

She had finished her knitted scarf and borrowed patterns and brought wool for more. Took a mini bus tour of the region, even considered a weekend in the snow laden ski fields in the nearby alpine resorts. But decided against it. She couldn't ski and knew from childhood memories it was much more fun throwing snowballs *with* someone.

Killing time and stifling her misgivings over

her friendship with Will, Hannah called in for chats with Mary in the op shop or annoyed Emma while she worked in The Stables. Even helped sometimes to make herself useful and they managed coffee and cake together at the bakery when Emma was free. Lovely to share girl time with a female of a similar age and have a genuine friend again. Who didn't whine about her problems or expect you to solve them.

Crumbs, she realised. Her younger sisters really were gormless. Every day here in Tingara it became clear the future path she must take. No reverting to old habits.

And then suddenly the subject of her every waking thought appeared at her door.

'Oh.' She opened to his knock one evening.

The exhibition was only days away. His paintings must be done. And he was here. They stared at each other stupidly for what seemed ages but in reality was only seconds.

'I missed you,' he said.

Thank God. 'Good.' Hannah grinned to herself as Will looked hurt by her blunt response until she added, 'I missed you, too.'

Having no idea of protocol in this situation, Hannah thought, *What the heck.* She cupped his cold face in her warm hands and gently kissed him. Then she wound her arms around his neck, pressing every inch of her body up hard against his.

'Kiss me senseless,' she begged.

Walking inside, bodies and mouths crushed together, Will kicked the door shut with his foot and proceeded to oblige her request.

For Hannah, all anxieties of recent days and memories of disagreements fell away in the heat of reunion. Telling Alma or not. Ginny's boasts about Will. Were they even true? All pushed aside. Blitzed by the pleasure of being with a chap who was fast becoming her world and desperately important in her life. Lots of potential hurdles, of course, but she wouldn't go there. Not tonight.

They moaned and kissed, and Hannah knew the burning explorations of Will's expert caresses on her warm skin. Wrapped and snuggled together before the fire on the sofa, Fluffy's usual place was relinquished to their visitor, the forbidden pet forced to curl up on a mat by the fire instead.

Later, Will said, 'Remind me never to disagree with you again or let you win.'

'That wouldn't be any fun. No making up afterwards.'

'True but you should know that, for the first time ever in my life, being without or away from someone made me feel lonely.'

'I'm afraid to think where we're going with this.'

'It will work out. Worrying won't change what's meant to be. So, are we still on for my exhibition opening this weekend?'

'Wouldn't miss it.'

Will arranged the same train and hotel for them, except for the addition of what he called necessary *glad rags* for opening night. So smart warm clothes found their way into overnight bags.

In Hannah's case, a pert little blue slinky number good as new she found with Mary's help in the op shop. She was finding with time on her hands to browse and shop on holiday, she revelled in unique if not the latest trendy gear. An uplifting change from the dark skirt suits and pumps she usually wore back home for work, donning any old casual thing when she was home.

By mid-July, the weather had turned deeply icy with sharp frosty mornings spreading their thick white crust on the ground. Cutting winds blew in, feeling as though they came directly off the Antarctic. People moved about less and tourist numbers dwindled during the week although at weekends travellers still braved the cold to visit. The ski fields higher up were busy.

On the day before Will's prestigious exhibition opening, he suggested taking Ginny's BMW from Tingara into Albury, this time for reliability in the chancy weather instead of *Dora* with the threat of light snowfalls forecast.

Still fearful of being behind the wheel, especially in such conditions, Hannah encouraged Will to drive, claiming unfamiliarity with the country back roads. He accepted her reason without question.

On arrival many hours further south in the city both appreciated the slightly milder climate by the sea. Next morning, Hannah thought Will surprisingly calm before his big event when they met in the hotel foyer to leave for the gallery.

Will's intense gaze all over her made her grow hot and red from blushing. 'Dynamite,' he murmured.

'You won't need it but good luck anyway,' she whispered.

Feeling adored and proud of the man at her side, they took a taxi to the reception. Already, parked cars lines all streets surrounding the gallery and when they entered, indoors was crowded, buzzing with conversation.

'Perry's ad campaign is a success then,' Will said wryly, a sparkle of quiet pride in his eyes.

Although impressed by the attendance, Hannah's gaze scanned the gallery walls, now covered with Will's impressive accomplished works. The moment Will appeared, Perry exclaimed and whisked him away. A strolling waiter pressed champagne into her hand. Alone now, she hovered in the background, studying the art loving guests. Some obviously wealthy, others purely art lovers. Collectors even. And shamelessly eavesdropped on their comments, mostly positive.

Soon after, Courtney and Lewis in tandem at

the door caught her eye across the room, waved and joined her. The women hugged in greeting, Lewis air-kissed.

Perry called order, welcomed everyone, introduced and praised Will, keeping his speech professionally short. Then the guest of honour was gone. From time to time, Hannah actually glimpsed a popular Will somewhere in the gallery spaces among the crowd.

Red dots began appearing on paintings and the siblings briefly had a chance to meet their brother when he joined them.

Hannah received a tender kiss on the cheek. 'Sorry for neglecting you,' Will managed before guests descended to invade the conversation and Perry dragged him away again.

'I am *so* proud of him,' Courtney leaned in to confide.

Hannah barely heard her comment above the drone of conversation.

'Aside from Lewis pulling apart computers and programming them from childhood, destined for IT, I *so* admire William for having the courage to follow his heart and passion. At the cost of our parents in his life.'

Hannah detected a note of envy in her voice. 'So, you're a full time mother?'

Courtney nodded. 'Charlotte is an adorable gem and we have a nanny. And of course I support Thomas in his career. With my family's connections, I'm quite the handy asset.'

Her musical laugh pretending to be carefree did not disguise the underlying note of what Hannah thought sounded like discontent in her comment. Perhaps her life at the moment, for all its privileges, was not completely fulfilling. Maybe she was just having a bad day.

Sensing her gloom, Hannah said, 'My sister Heather is a homemaker, too and loves it. She has two energetic pre-schooler boys, Andrew and James, and they certainly keep her busy. What's more important than motherhood and raising a family?'

'Self-esteem.'

Hannah sighed, knowing the struggle well. Although in her case, outside her job, it wasn't so much a lack of courage as a sense of direction and purpose.

'We're all bound to other things when we don't really want to be, aren't we? We all have our dreams.' She grew pensive. What were hers? Smiling, she asked, 'If you could do or be anything you wanted without any consideration to anyone else, what would it be?'

In recent weeks, she had asked herself the same question.

'Oh, my passion isn't a fantasy. I attended university. Mother presumed it was merely to fill in a few years until I married,' she said wryly, 'but I had other plans.'

Hannah picked up on her first comment. 'What did you study?'

'Fashion design and technology at a dedicated Villa Maison just out of Paris.'

'Sounds interesting.'

Courtney came alive and her enthusiasm burst. 'It was. They led us to be creative and curious. It was an exciting and varied programme. I loved it. It provided an environment like a working fashion studio. Sketching, colours, learning to build a collection. We attended exhibitions all over Europe. In third year, we focused on our own personal imprint and creating a portfolio. It was fabulous.' She sighed. 'But then I returned, met Thomas and married. One doesn't plan love.'

Too true, Hannah was forced to agree.

'I was given the wedding of the year among my parents' social set and mother warned me to only have the one child. Apparently, in her estimation, any more would cramp my lifestyle. She even told us where I should enrol my daughter in private school already. Poor Charlotte. She's barely two. I want her to have a childhood first. And can you imagine? She would be so lonely without siblings. At least William and Lewie and I had each other growing up while our parents were absent.'

After a few glasses of wine, Courtney's tongue knew freedom and Hannah let it run.

'So what *are* your plans?'

She wrinkled her nose. 'On ice at the moment but not forgotten. While I was at private school, so many of my friends came from families that didn't just write a cheque to pay the fees like mine but from families who had sacrificed everything so their daughter could attend. The girls might not have wanted designer clothes even if they could have afforded it but they were certainly looking for style and that little something different from their fashion. Yuppie clothes at a competitive price, if you like. It would be such a creative challenge to own a business that supplied that niche need.

'Oh. My. God.' Courtney spluttered on her wine. 'I don't believe it. William asked the olds? Now that's what I call *front*.'

Hannah followed the direction of her gaze as a distinguished older couple entered the gallery. Fashionably late. The unsmiling man acknowledged no one but the slim elegant woman flashed a creamy smile at everyone.

Will's parents!

Hannah cringed and shuffled awkwardly. 'Um...actually...I did. A neighbour gave me their address and I just popped an invitation in the post.' Alma did warn her she might regret it.

Courtney turned on her. 'Without his knowledge? Big mistake. He'll be furious.'

'It won't help mend bridges? Surely when they see-'

'Hannah, dear,' Courtney grabbed her arm and shook her head, 'trust me, it's the last thing in the world William would want.' Her lovely pencilled eyebrows dipped into a quick frown. 'Tell you what, I'll cover for you. Pretend I invited them. Love that outfit mother's wearing,' she muttered. 'Father won't speak to a soul. I best go rescue them.'

She wove her way through the lively chatting crowd, heading to where her parents stood like statues, casing the room. As Courtney reached them, she whipped a glass of wine and canapes from passing waiters and handed it to her parents, smiling and engaging them in conversation.

'I'll kill her.'

Hannah jumped at the voice in her ear and spun around, smiling at the brothers to cover her panic.

'They won't want to see me,' Lewis said, 'so I'm free and off.'

He dissolved into the crowd. Because he was gay? How sad and intolerant.

As though his radar had sensed his parents' arrival, Will stood rigid with fury at her side. He was never cross. Hannah wanted to sneak out a back door and disappear. Preferably on a plane back to England. What had she done?

'Who?' she squeaked.

'My bloody little sister.'

Hannah winced as he swore again. Another thing Will never did. 'Why?'

'For inviting my parents.'

'Well, this afternoon isn't invitation only.

Perhaps they heard about it somehow,' she managed an explanation.

Will irate was a scary sight and Hannah felt rotten knowing she was the cause. Hannah replaced her empty glass of champagne and grabbed another.

'Possible,' he growled, his voice low, 'but odd. I won't be speaking to them.'

Too late. Even as he spoke, Courtney and his parents turned in their direction. Bollocks.

Will stiffened even straighter beside her. For a moment he looked about to bolt but as his family wove closer there was no escape. To ignore them now would be the rudest of snubs and Hannah suspected Will, a product of his breeding, and against his every instinct, would play his part.

When Will's father extended a hand in greeting, his son's upbringing surfaced and he was forced to remove one of the hands he had deliberately thrust into his pockets to shake it. His mother leant forward, perhaps expecting an air kiss on the cheek but her son stepped back and merely nodded.

'Father. Mother,' he acknowledged tensely, as though they were royalty and had done him an honour by their presence.

Hannah watched on in silence, unsmiling and not daring to speak, feeling waves of leashed strain rise around them. She relaxed against Will when he slid an arm around her waist.

'It is my pleasure to introduce a dear friend of

mine, Miss Hannah Charles, out here in Australia for a few months from England. My parents, Judge William and Olivia Bennett.'

Polite greetings ensued after which Will's mother immediately pulled a tight smile and said crisply, 'So have you sold any of your little paintings, William?'

'Oh, yes, he has,' Hannah cut in, enthused on his behalf, 'there are little red dots everywhere.'

Will squeezed her and she caught his amused glance. Only then did she realise her mistake. His parents would know that. The comment was a sarcastic barb.

Will glared at his mother and without an ounce of emotion in his voice said, 'As Hannah mentioned, I have indeed. I've moved on from graffiti, mother,' he said smoothly. 'Incredible, isn't it to think I, of all people, your oldest son and heir, should be able to paint anything let alone sell it?'

'Will,' Hannah stood on tiptoe and looked over the crowd, 'I can see Perry over there. Do you think he needs you?'

He ignored her attempt at conciliation. His hand slid from her waist to entwine their fingers, giving them a gentle squeeze of understanding. He was playing the game.

Relentless and with admirable calm, he continued. 'Amazing, wouldn't you say to see how successful your children are despite your best efforts to stifle their dreams. Unless it was with your stamp of approval, of course. An architect, a computer genius and a daughter who impressed you by marrying an eminent surgeon. Fortunately, it was a union of love and not only to unite two powerful wealthy families.'

He didn't raise his voice so those crushed around them would never know in their midst was a family at conversational war. Will's comments were uttered with such quietly fierce control it was almost not a rebuke at all.

Before his shocked parents could respond, he grabbed Hannah's elbow and steered her away. 'Excuse us. I believe I prefer my brother's company. I notice you haven't spoken to him. Yet.' He mimicked his mother's tight smile. 'I'm sure he would appreciate it if you didn't completely ignore him as though he were a stranger and not your son.'

Chapter 11

Hannah felt awful for inciting antagonism in Will's family by inviting his parents. Even as she was being dragged away, she smiled at them and said tactfully, 'Thank you so much for coming. I understand you both have busy schedules.'

'I wonder why they *did* come,' Will frowned in suspicion.

'It's the weekend. They would have more free time, wouldn't they?' Hannah offered.

'Father never leaves his study at home or his room in chambers.'

Hannah disliked this side of him, surprised Will was still so affected by his past. In all his eco living, yoga, meditation, vegetable growing, peaceful lifestyle, she would have thought he could let go. Look ahead to the future and not back.

She had already decided she wasn't about to let Courtney take the blame for this misunderstanding over his parents' arrival but now was not the time to mention it. She would confess later. When tempers were less frayed.

'Did you notice Father didn't say a word? As usual. Just stood there like the superior being he believes himself to be. He saves speech for pontificating in court.'

Hannah was stunned by Will's deep resentment. 'Well you hardly gave him a chance,' she said lightly.

As the day progressed, and crowds came and went, an edgy Will returned to Hannah's side. 'Apart from my parents' unwanted visit, it's all going well. Show's on for a month. Perry wants me back here again soon but right now I need to leave. I don't do cities.'

'Me either.'

'I'll tell Perry we're leaving.' He ducked off.

Courtney it seemed was waiting for her moment. The instant Will moved away, she joined Hannah. 'You two okay?'

Hannah nodded. 'Why?'

'Don't tell William about inviting our parents today,' she warned. When Hannah would have objected, she added, 'It won't serve any purpose or make the slightest difference to him who tried to mend the rift, my stubborn brother would still have reacted the same way. Okay, our parents aren't perfect but whose are, right?'

Hannah considered that question and realised her own parents had come close. Yes, there had been the occasional tension. Rare. When her father disappeared into his garden shed and her mother furiously baked until he returned and somehow in unspoken understanding all would be well again. They had deeply loved and respected each other, and persisted to make their marriage work.

If she ever met *the right one*, Hannah knew, she would hope to create a similar deeply loving and solid family of her own, using her parents' example as role models.

Lewis joined them and when Will also returned to see his sister chatting to Hannah, he scowled. 'I'm not sure I'm speaking to you.'

'Nothing new in that,' she grinned. 'Hannah are you coming out to eat with Lewie and me? Will's sulking.'

'You know how I feel about them,' he retorted.

'Yes we do,' Lewis said dryly. 'You tell us often enough. Deep down you still hurt but you need to admit it before you can fix it.'

'We all grew up in the same house and situation, William,' Courtney said. 'Accept our parents for who they are, agree to disagree, be civil and move on. Hoping they'll change won't happen. You'll never have peace.' In the same breath, she went on easily, 'Coming Hannah? We'll drop you back at your hotel later.'

'Thanks. I'd love to. You be okay, Will?' She turned to him. Maybe he just needed time alone.

'Keep your hair on,' he groaned, 'I'm coming.'

Courtney gave a smug grin and high fived

with Lewis. 'Works every time, doesn't it, bro?'

He nodded. 'Where are we going?'

Courtney shrugged. 'Anywhere there's substantial food. You can only live on champagne and canapes for so long. Somewhere close? Let's walk and explore.'

Lewis fell in beside Will ahead, the brothers easily chatting.

'The folks invited us all back to the house,' Courtney said as they strolled along behind, rugged up against the chill.

'Even Will?' Hannah was amazed.

She nodded. 'Only a polite token gesture. They knew he would refuse. I said he was obliged to stay at the gallery and that Lewis and I had other arrangements. Well, we've made them now, haven't we?' she winked. Cheeky. So like Will. 'Besides, I can see them any time.'

Hannah raised amused eyebrows and grinned while Courtney stopped before a small café and peered through the door.

'Hey guys,' she called her brothers back, 'this place is humming. Always a good sign.' She scanned the menu board easel on the street. 'Food looks interesting.'

With no objections raised, they all found a table near the front window and ordered. Conversation started and centred on Will's exhibition but once the food and hot drinks appeared, it moved on to Courtney's brief mention earlier of her fashion boutique idea.

'You should just, like, totally do it, sis,' Lewis said eagerly, fluttering a hand in the air, then immediately began sketching plans on their paper serviettes.

Hannah grinned and shook her head. This family was so creative, it gave her a buzz just to be around them. And encouragement to pursue her own life more freely, too.

Will jumped aboard the discussion with his own suggestions. 'I can paint murals for your walls. Might need to be trendier than a landscape but I'm handy with graffiti, too.'

They all laughed. A family joke?

'Hey, that's not such a silly idea.' Courtney grew serious. 'But let's be realistic about all this. I need capital and I can't ask Thomas.'

'If you're connected to your husband in business as well as at home,' Lewis pointed out, 'it's a recipe for disaster and won't ever be totally yours.' He held up both hands as if being arrested. 'I know you'll fret about the fallout from the folks but your trust fund from grandfather has been sitting there for two years. Time to dip into it, hon.'

'I've already considered that but he was such a traditionalist,' she groaned.

'He was also an entrepreneur and a businessman. He researched his markets, thought outside the box and went with his gut,' Will said persuasively.

'You need to do all that stuff, sis,' Lewis said,

'and meanwhile scout for the right location. I can help you there. I know this guy in real estate. His finger is on the pulse of a trend before people even know about it.'

'All right,' Courtney said carefully, looking between her brothers. 'Good to know I have support.'

'I'll do all your web and marketing stuff. Leave it to me,' Lewis offered. 'Give me a name.'

'For the shop?'

'Boutique, honey.'

Courtney smiled. '*Simply Me.*'

'Simply catching.' Lewis beamed.

'Hannah's an accountant,' Will said warmly, glancing at her. 'Maybe she could give you some financial advice. While she's still here.'

'You're leaving soon?' Courtney sounded disappointed.

'No, of course not.' Hannah smiled, brushing aside Will's cryptic comment. 'I'm still here for about a month and I'm more than happy to help. British and Australian laws will differ but the principles and systems will be similar. Everything's global these days.'

'You guys have made me believe this can actually happen.' Courtney seemed in shock at the turn of conversation and pressed hands to her cheeks.

'*Make* it happen, Sis,' Lewis challenged.

Hannah already liked him. He was forthright and fun.

'Start sketching your designs, kiddo.'

'I have a million ideas and a bulging portfolio already created.'

'How about I come around to your place and you can show me,' Lewis said, 'then we'll approach manufacturers for stock and toss about some ideas on branding.'

Courtney laughed. 'Hold on. One thing at a time.'

'Don't let the grass grow.'

'Okay.' Courtney's enthusiasm bubbled. 'Right now?'

'Sure. If it suits.'

'Thomas is on late shift at the hospital. Stay for dinner? That includes Henry, too, of course. William? How about you and Hannah?'

'Sorry, Sis, we're booked to head back up country on the evening train again. Next time. When I don't have any pressure of an exhibition deadline. Not sure I'll do another one any time soon.'

'Stress isn't you, is it?' Courtney agreed and reached over to rest a hand on her brother's arm. 'You've been tense lately. Maybe *you* should consider a holiday,' she laughed, glancing toward Hannah.

Will chuckled, appreciating his sister's joke and the irony.

'Maybe Perry will consider your work on consignment as you produce it?'

'Already crossed my mind.'

'Hannah, it's been lovely to meet you,' Courtney said as they all rose. 'Will we see you again?'

'Not sure.'

With the late lunch and serviette scribbling done, the group said their goodbyes, hugged and parted.

Will and Hannah returned to the hotel to collect their bags and made it to the station in plenty of time. They each grabbed a hot drink to start the journey. At its end in Albury, they slid into the purring comfort of Ginny's BMW and set the heater going.

They were almost back to Tingara when Will said, 'There's going to be a break in the weather next week. Milder days. Interested in a hike into the foothills and an overnight camp out in a stockman's hut?'

'Won't it be too cold?'

'Yeah, walking will be chilly but it's only a few hours up and back to one of the lower ridges and the hut is basic but cosy.'

Hannah wavered, the suggestion pushing beyond her usual comfort zone.

'Be an experience,' Will appealed.

'Won't there be snow?'

'Only light, not deep. It's awesome country. Be a shame to miss it while you're here.'

He kept hinting at her departure when she was trying not to dwell on her holiday's end, drawing closer by the week.

'All right,' she agreed, grinning, 'I'll-'
'Do it?'
'Think on it.'
'We'll only have a brief window of opportunity. Clear days don't often happen up there.'

His demanding kisses goodnight were in utter contrast to the first tense time they returned from the city. Hannah was tempted to invite him to stay. The urge to be loved by him was so strong for both right and wrong reasons. She craved and adored him but also selfishly wanted to experience him as her lover. He would be slow and tender, creating unforgettable memories to take home. The unpleasant thought of leaving loomed in her mind like a nightmare so she shook it away.

'Sleep on it,' he murmured.

For a moment, playing catch up over her reflections, Hannah thought Will meant sleeping together! Wrong wave length.

'Oh. The walk. Sure. Can I come down for a cuppa in the morning? I have a couple things I need to talk to you about.'

Will looked intrigued. 'Any time.'

Two things played on her mind and she needed to clear them up before they took what she suspected might be the inevitable next step in their relationship.

'Thanks for everything.' He kept holding her in the porch, reluctant to let her go, and nuzzled her neck, creating delicious sensations through her body. 'The sibs love you to bits and the folks didn't terrify you.'

'Why should they? I don't know them. In my profession, I'm used to dealing with people and take everyone at face value.'

'Is that a subtle hint?'

'Courtney and Lewis had a point. Accept. Let go.' Sentiments that also carried meaning in her own life.

Will drew back from her, her face in shadow. 'I keep hoping they'll mellow.'

'You know them better than I do and whether that's even possible. Courtney doesn't agree.' She shrugged. 'People only change when they really want to.'

He reached out and his hand cupped her cheek. Hannah leant into it.

'Beautiful *and* clever.' He straightened, pressed his lips to hers with warmth and fire, and retreated down the steps. 'In the morning then?'

She nodded. He blew a kiss and she laughed. 'Just go.'

'You don't make it easy,' he called out as he grabbed his bag from the boot and walked back up the driveway toward the Lane and home.

Icy fingers of deep winter nipped at her bare face as Hannah strode briskly down the Lane next morning to Will's place in an effort to stimulate her circulation if not to keep warm. Will wanted to go on an overnight hike in this?

She wasn't sure he would appreciate the news she was about to break to him this morning but she needed to explain and clear her conscience for what she had chosen to do. She hoped he had slept well and was receptive after the pressure of recent weeks preparing for his exhibition. A situation by his own admission he usually chose to avoid. She admired his principles but sometimes life took over.

Feeling more at home each time she called, Hannah tapped on the French doors and let herself into the sunroom. The gorgeous furry tortoiseshell ball that was Callie curled on a sofa, dozing. No sign of easel or canvas in the room today.

'Will?' Peering through into the kitchen, she saw him brewing tea. 'Morning.' She sidled next to him and allowed herself to be thoroughly kissed.

With his arm still caressing her waist and back he said, 'Had breakfast?' She nodded. 'I should have invited you to share my French toast.'

'You should.'

He lowered his voice seductively. 'Or you could have just come home with me last night and stayed over and helped me make it this morning.'

Longing pulsed through her at his suggestion.

If she knew where it was, she was *so* tempted to drag this man off to his bedroom. 'I could.'

'Another time.'

'Definitely,' she whispered.

In order to get down to business, Hannah stepped away and settled on a stool. Despite their affection and warmth, still uneasy about the reason for this visit but only because she treasured her relationship with Will and her imminent admissions were a potential threat. She winced at the thought of placing it in jeopardy because of her crazy need for honesty. But if Alma ever said anything, Will would know it was because of Hannah's meddling.

'The usual?' Will asked. She nodded. 'I like the way you make yourself at home. And take advantage of me,' he grinned.

She scoffed. 'As if.' Then frowned. 'I'm not getting too pushy?'

He shook his head. 'You're not like that.'

Hannah loved their cheeky banter and Will's devilish mood made her approach easier. Any doubts were only in her own mind. Drawing from her parents' lifelong partnership, Hannah considered openness vital in a relationship.

Will poured her a steaming mug from the pot and pushed it toward her across the counter. Hannah removed her gloves and wrapped her hands around its heat. Her fingers tingled as sensation returned.

His soft brown eyes met her gaze. 'What's

up?'

Okay, straight into it then. 'Two things. Hear me out first?'

Will obviously caught the reservation in her voice because he leaned forward, arms folded on the counter and frowned. 'Am I so intimidating?'

'I care what you think.'

'Of you? Highly, if that's any consolation.'

Hannah looked down into her mug of tea, 'I told Alma that Bernie is dead,' she blurted out before she lost courage and then held her breath.

'Really,' he said quietly.

She looked up and caught his glare of disappointment. 'Alma wept with gratitude and thanked me.'

'Okay.' He paused. 'I'm surprised. I always had the impression she would rather keep the past buried.'

'Did she tell you that?'

'Obviously not,' he shrugged, 'or I would have been better informed. Confiding in another woman must make a difference.'

Will studied her, not the criticism she almost expected but rather a measure of concession and admiration.

Hannah related the essence of what she had researched and uncovered. Alma's belief that Martin might be interested to know what happened to his father. Where Bernie had been living and opal mining all those years. And old

George's comments and observations about his long-time mate.

'Just goes to show how wrong a man can be,' Will said.

'Do you mean yourself or Bernie?' Hannah teased.

'Both. You're a woman with a deep natural intuition and the courage to back it.'

Hannah wished she felt as strong as he claimed. 'Not always. I was wrong about you.'

'How?'

'That you weren't my type. My bad.'

'Pleased to hear it. Think what you would have missed out on. So…what's the other thing on your mind?'

'*I* sent the exhibition opening invitation to your parents.'

A whole range of emotions crossed his face. Disbelief. Shock. 'Why would you possibly think I'd want them to attend after I explained our family situation?'

'I wanted you to have a close family like me.'

Will scoffed. 'Well, thanks for the sentiment but not for interfering. Did it do any good? Was it worthwhile? Did you achieve your purpose?'

Hannah understood and absorbed his frustration. 'No.'

'Of course not. Now you've met my parents you can see reconciliation is impossible.'

Yet you still hope, she thought sadly. 'Don't you ever want to sit down and talk to them about it?'

Will slowly shook his head and pulled the hint of a wry smile. 'Their principles are set in stone and never open for discussion.' He snapped a short laugh. 'Ironic, isn't it, in the light of my father's profession where he's obliged to consider both sides of a case.'

'Then I'm truly sorry for you and trying to help. In all conscience, I couldn't let Courtney take the blame.'

'Fair enough. If it's any consolation, deep down I still wish my parents' dynamics were different but my sibs are right. I need to rise above that dream or the past will control my future.' He paused. 'I'd like to be closer to my family and you're too close.'

Hannah stiffened. 'Excuse me?'

'Well it sounds like you're so involved with your sisters' lives that it borders on meddling obsession.'

It was Hannah's turn to be stunned by Will's blunt remark. 'Actually it's not.' She smarted. 'But I can see how an outsider might read it that way. We all care about each other and, admittedly, probably too much but we've talked over and shared stuff all our lives.' She shrugged. 'Women chat and confide more anyway. When our parents were still alive, our mother was the listener. After she died, I guess as the oldest, I kind of fell into that role. By default,' she pointed out. 'Not necessarily by choice.'

They stared at each other long and hard. Each with unresolved family issues within themselves. In her own case, when to cut and run? And more importantly, how to move on. Where? Alone? With someone else? So many questions and possibilities, Hannah's head was spinning.

Suddenly the future was closer than she wanted. Her holiday in Tingara was slipping by. She needed to figure out her true emotions for Will. What she would return to in England.

After a while, Will observed quietly, 'There's a lot we don't know about each other.'

Oh God, was he about to dump her? Even the thought of the likelihood was devastating. The reality would be unbearable. 'And some stuff still to fix,' she admitted bravely.

'And work out what's between us?' he suggested.

Hannah's whole body sagged with relief. That sounded hopeful, not fateful, and privately acknowledged that was the biggie for them.

'Maybe that long hike will give us more time to get acquainted.'

The cheeky grin that accompanied his olive branch crumbled the tension in the air that rose from their mutual brutal honesty. At least it appeared they were still talking and friends.

'You're determined to get me out in this weather.'

'It's only a couple hours up. A steady climb then the ridge. We'll keep below the snowline then its easy walking to the hut. I have all the gear but we'd need to consider it in the good weather break in the coming days. Decided yet?'

Hannah sighed deeply with misgiving but knew she could place her trust in this man. And it would mean being alone together.

'I've walked the Cotswold hills around our village and once or twice in light snow. I'm not a novice and you sound like an experienced bushwalker, so I guess I'm up for it.'

Will beamed an infectious smile that promised emotional danger. His spark of vitality that he rarely revealed shone through, lighting up his face and lending a glitter of triumph to his dark brown eyes. His excitement transferred to Hannah. His reaction, as though he had just won a major battle or the lottery, cracked through his usual placid façade.

A buzz of anticipation and the unknown drummed through them both. Each thinking their own deep thoughts, minds alive with expectation.

He became all lively action. 'We'll need to leave at dawn. It's an hour drive up to the trail carpark in the national park. The only unknown threat will be the changeable weather but we'll be prepared for that. I know the track and places to shelter if necessary before we reach the hut.'

'This is your country. I trust you. I've trudged

in snow.'

'We won't be in the high country or the alps. They're under deep snow at this time of year. The lower track where we'll be hiking is well defined and signposted.' He hesitated. 'Do you mind if we take the BMW again? *Dora* would struggle up those hills,' he admitted sheepishly.

'As long as you drive.'

'Sure. You go fish out your warmest hiking gear. I have waterproofs and boots you can borrow, depending on the fit. I'll start filling our backpacks with a bedroll, basic food, safety equipment and medical supplies.'

'Sounds serious.'

'Need to be prepared. I'll bring over some boots for you to try in the morning. If they're a no-go, we'll head into the camping store in town. Norm stocks everything. We should leave the day after.'

And so it was. One pair of boots fitted comfortably. Another female's surplus perhaps? Hannah laid out a change of spare clothes plus what she would wear tomorrow. And waited.

Sleep eluded her but it hardly mattered. Her body ran on adrenalin from the anticipation of not only the hike but the next logical step she hoped she would take with Will in their relationship.

She didn't commit easily but every nerve in her body was strung so tight she needed it to happen or she would explode.

With Will's exhibition safely launched and underway, Hannah privately vowed her remaining precious weeks in Tingara would be wisely used.

Chapter 12

Daybreak spread pale gold light through the bare branches and glowing beams down the Lane, marking the start of a new and special day. Will arrived, hair tied back, beanie pulled down snugly about his ears so that only his beautiful smiling face was visible.

When he kissed her, his cold lingering lips promised much more.

He loaded their packs into the boot of Ginny's car, checked and approved her hiking clothes, then said, 'Let's away.'

The one hour drive from town and up winding mountain tourist roads to the carpark where they would leave the vehicle overnight, passed in a charged but companionable silence.

Alighting into the crisp fresh air of the slightly higher altitude, securing their packs, locking the car, for Will was all about business. Hannah respected he knew his terrain and co-operated with his comments and instructions.

The first leg of their day's walk was a slow steady rise through a tall forest of peppermint eucalypts winding alongside a gully creek. They spoke little, finding their pace, Will leading but constantly turning back to check on Hannah. She was invigorated, content, occasionally warning him with 'Kodak moment,' and stopping for photos. He had assured her it was an easy gradual climb today with a midday picnic stop so they took their time.

Bracken filled the gullies and created a thick understorey in the bush. They stopped for water and trail snacks, dipping their hands into the rushing icy waters of bubbling streams and refilling drink bottles.

Hannah started out feeling cold but the exercise soon made her body hum with warmth.

'Powerful country,' she said as they perched on a lichen covered boulder to take their mid-morning rest.

'Invigorating in winter. Stunning in spring and summer.'

Hannah wondered if Will's hint was a feeler when he mentioned such impossibilities for her to see and experience. He well knew she wouldn't be here in spring or summer. Unless she stayed on or returned, was he probing to get a response, sound out her plans? How could she when she was undecided herself?

Honestly, at this point in her life and prompted by Will's example and guidance and teachings in his life that gave her pause for thought in her own, she was open to any situation or development once her old life in

England was sorted.

It really depended on what developed with Will, conversations that might be started with him. Because they shared deep feelings and much more.

With this quietly strong scrummy man for over two months now – where had they gone? – she had learnt loads. Such a surprise. Welcomed into his group of close friends. Become acquainted with his neighbours, in particular Alma Powell of course who had become like a favoured aunt, whose confidences Hannah dearly treasured for the balance it brought to her own life since the death of her parents.

She had personally grown in Will's friendship and affections. Recognised the shake up her life needed. Was falling in love with the man responsible for it all in the best way, but she also knew the pitfalls ahead because they lived on opposite sides of the world.

As the days of her holiday too swiftly dwindled, even the smallest obstacle loomed larger in her mind. Who knew her holiday in Tingara would reap such a generous awakening and bring such a smashing chap into her life who, in the best and worst way, was far beyond a holiday romance.

Genuine deep feelings had built within her for weeks now, made all the more frustrating because of her looming departure. She could be practical, keep her distance from Will and play it safe but as the days passed, Hannah decided she would just go for it. Worry in advance only made her feeling more unsettled. If she blanked out the cons and just focused on *being* when she was with Will, she had to place her belief in fate and a bit of *qué será*. She only knew in her heart that this man was worth any risk she was prepared to take. She was trusting herself to him on this hike, wasn't she? And would willingly give her all to him if he asked. She was *that* invested in this romance.

Hannah's thoughts and steady tramping along the trail were interrupted when Will tossed back over his shoulder, 'Are you still with me back there?'

'On your heels.'

'Lunch stop down there.'

He pointed toward a torrent of water gushing down a gully, flowing beneath a timber foot bridge that led to an open but sheltered and grassy picnic area with a fireplace and tables below. Preoccupied in thought, Hannah hadn't realised they were descending.

Minutes later, it was a relief to shrug the pack from her shoulders. With no other hikers or campers about they enjoyed the surrounding virtual silence of open forest candlebark gums from which wallabies emerged to investigate but kept their distance. Will built a fire and filled the tin billy she had seen and heard swinging and clanging from his backpack all morning with icy clear water from the creek, settling it over the flames to boil for a cuppa and their packets of dry soup for lunch.

Hannah gaped when he produced a small and crusty baked Vienna loaf.

'That smells fresh.'

'Nipped down to the bakery early this morning.'

'We're hardly roughing it,' Hannah chuckled.

'That wasn't the idea. It's about the experience.'

'And memories?'

'Those too.'

Hannah hoped they would make more than memories tonight. Crumbs, she was getting right horny. From his words and actions, she trusted Will felt the same. Well, she would find out later wouldn't she?

'Your cheeks are flushed,' Will observed as he added hot water to their soup mugs to steep and thicken. 'Maybe sit back a bit from the fire?' He sliced the bread into chunks with a camping knife.

'Oh, right.' Hannah shuffled further away with embarrassment.

Had Will guessed and his comment was only a tease? For a while she didn't dare look at him. Just stared into the fire cupping her hands around her mug and nibbling the fresh bread.

'Nothing like bush tucker,' Will murmured, sitting alongside her, slurping his soup. 'Are you okay?' She nodded. 'For a wisp of a thing, you're stronger than you look.'

'I've walked parts of the Cotswold Way back home. It's right on our doorstep, after all.'

'I've heard it's steep in parts.'

'Can be. There are circular walks you can do and shorter easier sections. And wonderful views of the whole countryside from the escarpment. You can walk it year round but late spring and summer are the best times, of course, to see the wildflower meadows and beech woodlands rich with bluebells and the scent of wild garlic. The National Trails pass through the best landscapes. Picturesque villages, beautiful old churches and houses.'

'No such scenery here and the main colour is green,' Will said wryly.

Hannah smiled. 'True, but it's majestic. Breathtaking.' Her gaze rose skyward searching between the treetops for small patches of grey blue sky.

'The trail opens up this afternoon as we head for the ridge.'

They lingered a while before Will rose, repacked his gear and doused their fire.

'Onward and upward.' He shrugged on his pack and reached for her hand.

Slipping her fingers into his, Hannah said, 'Thanks for lunch.'

'You're welcome.'

He tugged her closer for a kiss, tucking a long

errant strand of her hair back beneath her fluffy pink beret again.

'Has your holiday achieved what you hoped?' he asked as they walked together back over the bridge and climbed to join the trail again.

'You sound like it's over. I have weeks yet. And to answer your question, yes, I believe it has resolved most issues for me. But also raised others.'

'Such as?'

'You,' she admitted softly.

'Am I a problem?' His fingers tightened in hers and his voice grew warily husky.

'More a...surprise.'

'Because?'

They stopped walking and faced each other.

Hannah hesitated. 'I never expected...romance.'

'That's one experience in life over which we have little control. The person. The attraction.'

'It excites and bothers me.'

'Feeling's mutual. If we stay here,' he drawled, 'I'll ravish you on the ground. Let's keep walking and we'll discuss this tonight?'

It was the first time they had addressed their feelings. 'Sure.'

But first Will slid his hand up into her hair and kissed her with deep hunger. Hannah felt like weeping with happiness and the promise of what lay ahead. Will released a long sigh before moving on and tugging her to follow.

Walking single file again on the trail, the afternoon brought another steady but manageable climb. Will led, clearly in no mind to rush for they often stopped to catch their breath and admire the emerging mountain views. He was right. It *was* all about the experience, surrounding nature, the sound of running water in creeks, sometimes close, sometimes distant in the bush. And rocky outcrops where they rested, snacking on handfuls of trail mix and refreshing gulps of cool water.

By late afternoon, the trees thinned so that by the time the track crested the plateau, clear spectacular vistas of the Australian Alps spread out all around them. Hands on hips, Hannah gaped in wonder as they stopped for another breather, a stiff playful wind whipping about, tossing her hair.

'Come spring,' Will stretched his arms wide, 'all this will be a sea of alpine flowers.'

There it was again, this promise of a future she possibly would not see. Hannah ignored the small niggling twinge of regret to admire the never ending sky turning pale and grey with the lowering sun. The distant mountain scenery quietly proclaimed its majesty, giving inspiration to the soul. Tranquillity and beauty echoed everywhere.

Moved by the vastness of it all and the man who had invited her up here to share, tears began to skim down Hannah's cheeks. She sniffed and sighed.

Will glanced at her, frowning in concern. He slid off his own pack then helped Hannah with hers, wrapping an arm about her shoulder, drawing her close.

'It's been a long day and we've walked a fair distance. If you've had enough, we can safely camp out here just below the rise. We don't need to make it to the hut tonight.'

'Oh no. No.' He misunderstood. Hannah smiled through her tears and swiped at them. 'I've actually never felt so alive and happy. Inside, you know? Like my whole life has come to this pinnacle right at this moment in time. Thank you,' she swept her arms out, 'for showing me all this.'

'You don't regret it, then, the hike?'

Hannah turned to him, their faces close, noses almost touching. 'I wouldn't trade a single moment of today or experience of my time here, in Tingara and Australia, and with you. I'll remember them for the rest of my life.'

'I hope the memories we're making together don't end. Just yet. Life doesn't always fall into place for us the way we want or plan. Often it's simply about the moment.'

'So I'm discovering,' she whispered.

Will grabbed the ends of her thick scarf in his hands and hauled her, aligned, against him. A rush of cold wind swept over them as they kissed but neither noticed. Hannah shivered. Not from the sudden icy chill but the unspoken promise of more between them that made words unnecessary.

'What was that for?' she breathed afterwards.

'You simply must stop looking so adorable.'

'In these thick clothes and with a hat pulled down over my ears?' Hannah tipped back her head and laughed. 'Oh!' She blinked. 'It's snowing!'

She held out her hands and stuck out her tongue to catch a flake.

Will scanned the horizon. 'Weather's turning with nightfall. Best head for the hut. It's only another half hour.'

'This is just like home,' Hannah beamed with excitement as they loaded their packs again.

'Do you miss it?'

'England? No, actually,' she said with conviction as they briskly moved off along the top of the ridge, exposed to the light snowy onslaught, following orange track markers to the hut.

With the snow laden front moving in, they picked up their pace walking side by side, coat hoods up against the dusting of white swirling around them in flurries.

'Any chance of being snowed in, then?' Hannah asked cheekily, raising her voice against the elements as they trudged on.

'Nice thought,' Will chuckled, 'but this light

drift will probably be melted by morning. It wasn't forecast but these mild changes can blow up at any time and are over soon enough.'

'Bollocks,' Hannah muttered.

'It's the heavy storms we need to watch.'

The hazy view off to one side now with the incoming blustery weather cloud was like a thick fog and blocked out much of the remaining daylight.

Hannah was about to ask how much further when their destination gradually became visible ahead. A tiny timber hut of simple pioneering construction with a tin roof, and chimney at one end, that fitted perfectly into its landscape.

'What a little rustic gem,' Hannah said. 'How do we get in?'

'It's unlocked.'

Will stamped his boots under the small porch that sheltered the only door with one small window either side. When he pushed it, the door creaked and opened. Hannah followed.

Inside was basic and rustic with a small emergency stack of firewood and kindling.

'It's cute and dry.' Hannah turned a full circle as they shrugged off their packs.

Will busied himself making a fire. 'Unpack your bedroll and the food supplies and billy in my pack if you wouldn't mind.'

Hannah glowed in Will's strong reassuring company, removed her boots and padded about the hut in thick socks, helping set up in their cosy mountain refuge for the night.

'Any other hikers likely?' she asked.

'Not usually in winter but always possible.'

They shared a grin and Hannah prayed for continued solitude and privacy. Just her luck when she wanted Will to herself that fellow hikers might arrive at any moment, although they hadn't encountered anyone at the picnic area at lunch and only two others hiking in the opposite direction all day.

With the fire built, the dry logs snapped and took hold, licked by flames. Snug warmth filled the hut, Hannah and Will seated on the floor together arms wrapped around their knees before it while the billy sang on its way to a boil and their dried stew soaked in water to rehydrate.

'What's for dinner?'

'Kind of bean and vegie mince stew and I'll toss in a handful of rice to the billy when it's boiled, too.'

'Whatever it is after hiking all day will be wonderful.'

'We can toast the leftover bread in the morning and I have powdered milk for cereal or muesli for breakfast.'

Hannah cast her gaze at the flickering shadows leaping across the hut walls. 'Are there many of these in the mountains?'

'Couple hundred as I understand it all over the alpine regions here on the mainland and down on the island of Tasmania too. The original ones were for the early cattle men and women grazing stock up here. Gold miners, too, later on. These days, they're mostly used by skiers and bushwalkers.'

When the food was ready, he said, 'Eat first, talk later?'

Hannah nodded. 'I'm starving.'

The sounds of croaking frogs and scratching possums scuttling on the roof came to them as they ate their simple hot meal. Afterwards, Will surprised her by producing the makings for the treat of smores.

'You hid these in your pack?' Hannah laughed with delight, punching him playfully on the arm.

'Perfect camping food.'

With the marshmallows toasted over the coals and squished between chocolate coated biscuits, they indulged.

'How did they get to be called smores?' Hannah asked, swiping the soft oozing marshmallow with her tongue and licking delicious melting chocolate from her fingers.

'Wanting to know the answer to that I Googled.'

'As you do. And?'

'The first ever recorded recipe was known as Some Mores and is printed in a tramping and trailing book for girl scouts from 1927.'

'Impressive. So grateful some bright inventive

spark has left such a brilliant foody legacy.'

When Will suddenly went quiet, Hannah turned to him and caught his stare.

'What?' she asked warily.

'You have chocolate, here.' He reached over and laid a hand beneath her chin, brushing his thumb across her cheek. 'And on the corner of your mouth,' he added, leaning in to kiss it away.

Hannah happily participated in the moment which turned passionate and stirred every reaction from her body.

'So, is this why you brought me here?'

'To take advantage of you? Absolutely,' he drawled, 'but also because I wanted more time with you.'

'Me too,' she agreed softly.

'Explore these feelings. See where they lead,' he murmured. 'Get to know each other more.'

'Uh huh.' Because in her mind the leap of faith was still huge, she hesitated to begin talking about herself. 'Tell me all about Will Bennett. From childhood up and don't leave out a thing.'

'Best get comfortable then.'

He opened their bedrolls and they wrapped themselves up in them by the open fire, snuggled close.

'I was born and grew up in Tingara, of course, as you know. Trying to live up to my parents' high expectations. But I was unhappy, not succeeding. Everything they wanted me to do, I didn't. They were dictating my path in life and I resisted. So by the time I was a teen, we lived in Melbourne and I attended an exclusive private school. I was independent and defiant and clashed with my parents. Didn't want the life they wanted for me. University, a professional career. To *be* somebody important.

'My standards of success were different so I rebelled. I joined a graffiti gang to express my love for art. Fellow privileged mates like me with a bad attitude.'

He had mentioned the graffiti thing before and his mention of it now piqued Hannah's interest again.

'After a couple of close calls, I was eventually caught again, charged, cautioned and my spray cans confiscated.'

Hannah leant her head on his shoulder. 'So what happened?'

'Not proud of myself back then. My case went to court. Dad refused to help me or use any influence.' Will shrugged. 'Might sound a bit harsh but rightly so, I guess. I had to clean up my work and pay a fine. At which point my parents disowned me. Said they weren't wasting any more time and money on my education. So I finished secondary school and left.

'Had no idea where I wanted to go or what I would do. Headed north along the coast, lived rough, got work and learnt hard and fast about responsibility. Finally realised my parents' efforts weren't maybe so much about ambition but providing an opportunity for me which I eventually understood and appreciated but it still hurt to be pretty much banished from the family.

'I know my folks had committed heavily financially sending me to private school but I wanted to live and survive and earn my own way, and not in the city. I didn't see the reasoning in punishing someone for loving something. In my case, art, but a couple years down the track when I stopped feeling sorry for myself and resentful, I grew up and got it.

'So I decided that since art was what I loved, instead of doing it in the wrong places with the wrong crowd, why not make money out of it. I bought paper and created art and sold it to mates and friends. That was the start of making money to put myself through art school and architecture at university on the Gold Coast.

'I did architectural design over three years then another two years of masters where you get to specialise. I chose sustainable design. Its research based where you investigate and analyse in your field of choice. Once qualified you focus on a building aspect or design. I wanted to be my own boss, a general practitioner, for the freedom. It's an entry level qualification in the profession.'

As Will talked, Hannah absorbed it all, stared

into the flames, feeling the comforting vibrations from his murmuring voice as he spoke.

'So I worked and surfed,' he continued. 'Built my reputation, specialised in sustainable housing, especially for people out in the coastal hinterland up there in Queensland.'

'So how did you end up back here?'

'I was on a travelling and surfing trip with mates in May one year and visited the high country harvest festival in Tingara. Saw all the artisans and crafts people like Emma doing great stuff. I had some art work with me so I set up a random market stall and sold everything. I was so blown away, I decided to stay on for a while, get reacquainted with my old home town and planned on re-joining my mates when they headed back north again in a few weeks.'

'But you stayed.'

Will nodded. 'About five years ago now and I have no regrets. I bought my block of land in Gum Tree Lane cheap and, over a couple years, built myself a mud brick solar home.

'I lived in an old shed on the property. As it happens, it's now the chook shed and the poultry have made it their own these days but it was in much better condition when I was in residence.'

'You have a beautiful home and garden now,' Hannah said with admiration. 'It must have taken a heap of work.'

'Labour of love.' He humbly brushed aside

her praise then admitted, 'Family hasn't played a role in my life much in the past. My friends and sibs have been my family.'

'Do you see that changing in the future?'

'You've met my parents. Possibly not. Unless they mellow or I can face them without regret.'

'You seem so calm and together I'm surprised you haven't already.'

'It will happen one day when it's meant to. Ironically, maybe with more grandchildren. Mother's quite involved with Charlotte but Courtney knows her own mind and strongly voices it. I gather mother's learning to concede. My idea of a family will bear no resemblance to my parents', that's for sure, but I realise it's a big ask to expect a woman to settle down in a small country town.'

'Females your age are scarce in Tingara.'

'They happen along,' Will chuckled.

'But don't necessarily stay,' Hannah noted.

'True.'

Silence dropped between them as they both reflected for a moment on the meaning behind their conversation.

'Warm enough?' Will asked after a while.

'Mm, lovely and cosy listening to the wind out there.'

'It's not as wild as it can be up here. It will ease by morning.'

'I feel so comfortable in the hut it's hard to believe we're so isolated.'

'Nature's good for the soul.'

'Yes, after getting to know you I'm realising that. Dragging me outdoors every chance you get,' she teased.

'Seems to be working. You're more relaxed since your arrival. You were unwell and stressed from your life back home.' He paused. 'So, tell me all about you now,' he prompted.

Chapter 13

'Okay.' Hannah reflected a moment while Will added more logs to the fire then resettled beside her.

He waited expectantly.

'I've lived in Gloucestershire all my life. I love it but I don't believe I've fully appreciated all it has to offer. I've taken it for granted,' she admitted. 'The wider Cotswold Hills are littered with villages of picture postcard honey-coloured cottages. Small bridges over brooks, plants and flowers everywhere. The wealthy often have second homes there.' She glanced aside to Will. 'In my village of Snowshill the streets were used for filming the movie Bridget Jones' Diary.'

'Really?' Will's eyes glazed over. Clearly he had never heard of it and no idea what she was talking about.

'Just a small claim to fame.' Hannah thoughts turned reminiscent as she gazed at the low flames leaping around the new logs. 'It's charming and unspoilt with rows of pretty cottages. Quiet. Less busy than the more touristy surrounding towns. The medieval manor house is the main attraction. There's a central stone church and just outside the village fields of wild poppies, grazing sheep, and ripening grain in summer. The man who restored the manor house planted lines of lavender fields. Over thirty acres I think.'

'Sounds idyllic.'

'There's a pub but no shops. We drive into Broadway for that about ten minutes up the road.' Hannah slowly shook her head. 'I can't believe how hard I pushed myself before I came here. Weekend shopping and cleaning, sorting out my sisters' lives and dramas, listening and giving advice they never took. Leaving me without a life of my own. My fault,' she confessed. 'I made myself a martyr. I've learnt loads from you and slowed down on this holiday. I don't hear from Chelsea as much. At first what I thought was a crazy distance from England to travel has actually proved to be cathartic. And healing on many levels.

'Until I came here and met you I never stopped long enough to think. Coming from a working class family, I paid my own way through university. Worked jobs in Oxford between lectures and assignments.'

'That's because you're conscientious,' Will said. 'Maybe too much so.' When she grimaced, he added, 'An observation and compliment. Probably makes you your own worst enemy.'

'I'm starting to get that. My two younger

sisters are always bleating about my posh job.' Hannah frowned. 'I haven't heard from them lately. Odd. They're both probably engrossed with their latest boyfriends.

'Heather fell in love with Michael at high school and only ever wanted to get married and have kids. Victoria and Chelsea wanted the opposite. They live and work in London and rarely come home. Vic is a café and pub waitress. Lots of temporary and part time jobs. She's tall, leggy and blonde and targets rich boyfriends. Receives expensive gifts, is whisked off for holidays to gorgeous locations.

'Chelsea has always been a bit whacky and wild. Loves fashion. I bought all my sisters a necklace and earring gift set from Emma at The Stables. Chels works in an exclusive upmarket London boutique. Somehow always manages to turn up quirky finds in Covent Garden and Harrods. She knows where it's all at. She raves about Oxford Street and all the luxury window shopping and extravagant retail therapy to be had in Bond Street and Mayfair. I don't know how she affords it on her salary but I suspect each current boyfriend indulges her. They were invited to some film star's private yacht in the Mediterranean one year through a friend of a friend, you know?'

'Envious?' Will chipped in.

'Absolutely not. That kind of life doesn't interest me. All that Carnaby Street stuff with designer names and bars and pubs.' She wrinkled her nose. 'Not my scene at all. Our poor Dad with five women in the house and one bathroom. Heather and I shared a room but each of the younger girls had one of their own. When Heather married, it was the first time I had a room to myself.' Hannah couldn't help but turn reflective and not a little sad again as she spoke of it all. 'Since the day both our parents died, I've had the whole lonely place to myself.'

'Whoa. Back up there. Both your parents died at the same time?'

Hannah felt so comfortable chatting to Will she forgot herself and let slip more than she intended. Startled to realise her mistake, she gave a bleak nod.

'What happened?'

'Road accident.'

Will reached out and clasped her hands between his own. 'I'm so sorry. That must have been awful for you. I know you mentioned they died but not that it was together.'

Hannah shrugged, trying to appear brave. 'It's okay. I'm slowly coming to terms.' Stretching the truth there a bit.

'Want to talk about it?'

'I can't.'

Hannah felt him watching her for a moment. 'Maybe you should.'

'Please don't make me,' she moaned.

'You'll have to confide and trust someone

eventually.'

'I'm sure you're right but not tonight, okay?'

'Any time you need to talk-'

'Thanks but I won't.'

Hannah shut down, disappointed she couldn't talk more openly to Will. Frightened yet encouraged to find herself tempted to confide in him. So far she hadn't even told her sisters her deepest fear. But Will's warm easy manner was empowering and she edged closer to discussing that fateful night. She had been so close to blurting it all out but, bollocks, something still held her back. If she told anyone, she acknowledged it might just be him.

'I don't like to think of you keeping something big inside. Promise you'll try and tell me before you go?'

A big ask but she felt able to nod her assent, on the verge of tears, feeling ready to crumble, but she didn't want to spoil this special promising night together up here in the mountains.

Will's natural compassion surfaced as he watched Hannah struggle with her emotions. She sensed he wanted her to unburden the weight on her mind and she ached with love for him as a result.

They turned to each other, instinctively reaching out in this vulnerable moment, bedrolls shrugged aside, hands exploring, drawing close, lips finding what felt like home. Passion and need built, driving Hannah crazy.

'Could anyone just walk into this hut?' she whispered between kisses.

'At this late hour I doubt it,' he assured her. 'No sensible hiker would be walking in the dark in snow.' He slid one hand into her hair, cupped her head in his palm with the other and drew her closer. 'Let's crack open this tension, shall we, and live dangerously anyway?'

'You read my mind.'

Hannah was beyond caring. She just needed to express her feelings for this incredible man.

Coming down from the high later, the world remained suspended as they glowed with contentment and deep kissing.

Eventually, Hannah stirred enough to say, 'I can say with absolute truth that no one has ever made me feel *so much.*'

Will drew her tightly against him and into his arms, chuckling. 'It was damn good, wasn't it?'

'Nothing short of incredible. Eleven out of ten. Well done you,' she murmured, kissing his bare chest beneath her cheek.

'I've never wanted to *give* so much but you made it easy, you beautiful soul.'

Hannah shivered and Will drew the tumbled bedroll over them.

'I think we should do that again before morning.'

'Whenever you're ready,' she grinned and settled easily into a doze.

As it happened, they didn't wait long.

Afterwards, Will complained, 'I won't have enough energy tomorrow even walking downhill.'

'Goose,' Hannah laughed, raising herself on an elbow. 'You had plenty just now.'

She brushed back strands of his long and soft wavy hair and leant down, claiming ownership to kiss the warm lips that had paid so much of her body homage and, as a result, produced loads of delights.

Amid their loving, Hannah had thought but not spoken the words of love that snapped so easily to mind. The chemistry with Will was undeniable and sparked from their first meeting. She adored this man, which meant she was in deep trouble because as her reality kicked in, leaving him to return to England would be next to impossible. Her desires and feelings were *that* strong.

As Will drifted into sleep beside her, Hannah tried to do the same, denying future problems, feeling Will's warmth against her, aware of his steady breathing. The next thing she became aware of was the pale morning light and Will stirring beside her, kissing her awake.

'Morning beautiful sleepyhead.' He rose and dressed, adding wood to revive the embers and trotting over to the tiny window, peering outside. 'Snow's stopped.'

Hannah yawned and stretched. 'I'm too lazy

to move. All your fault for making me feel so scrummy.'

Will gave a dangerous chuckle, pushing back a mop of waves from his face and tucking it behind an ear. 'My pleasure.'

Hannah just wanted to strip his clothes from that gorgeous body and do it all again. She sighed instead. 'Oh I can assure you it was mine, too. What's for breakfast?'

'Cheeky. Cereal with powdered milk, toast and a hot cuppa when the billy boils.'

Reluctantly, Hannah dressed, rolled up their beds and began to tidy and pack while Will produced food. Ravenous, she took a second helping of everything he offered. They sat by the fire, nursing mugs of tea, letting the coals die down ready for dousing before they left.

Will put their small amount of rubbish into a bag to take off the mountain with them. They shrugged on their packs, took one last look around the hut to make sure all was as they found it, taking their memories with them.

'Ready?' Will drawled, taking her hand and a kiss.

She nodded. 'At least it's mostly downhill today, right?'

The sky was partly cloudy but clear above them as they crunched across the thin layer of snow, already melting at its edges. The wind had dropped as they strode into rhythm, the rocky trail wide enough to walk together.

Neither spoke their thoughts but Hannah had already determined that she would live for each moment of her remaining holiday, setting aside the future for now, refusing to let any concerns spoil her time with Will.

By late morning when the path narrowed and wound around rocky outcrops and huge boulders, they tramped single file again, Will leading. He moved on ahead and disappeared around a corner. Unconcerned, because they always caught up with each other again eventually, Hannah paused to snap a photo through the bush while the sunlight streamed across it and lit a waterfall in the gully below.

She continued on, keeping her camera handy because at certain moments the light could be awesome.

Rounding the bend, she noticed Will lying on the ground. For a moment she thought he had taken a break and was resting because his head lay on his pack. Was he letting her catch up? But he didn't move and he had an arm across his eyes.

Reaching him, she removed her pack and knelt alongside, grabbing his coat lapels. 'Will?' No response. 'Bollocks. What do I do?' she spoke out loud, her voice echoing through the silent bush, quickly scanning him for any external sign of blood or injury.

Then he moved and groaned. 'You kiss me better.'

Hannah's body sank with relief. He was teasing. Annoyed at playing an unkind trick, she punched him lightly. 'Nice one. You're faking.'

He struggled to sit up, wincing and grabbing his right foot. 'Actually I'm not. I was admiring that waterfall and caught the side of my foot between these boulders.' He frowned. 'I should have been more careful.'

'Can you walk?'

'Don't know yet.' He removed his pack and tried standing but his eyes crinkled shut in pain. 'Might need to strap it up. First aid kit's in the outside pocket of my pack.'

Together they tightly bandaged his ankle and she helped him try to stand again. He hopped and softly cursed.

'Might take a couple painkillers. Sorry but I'm going to slow us down.'

'We can take breaks.'

He eyed her strangely for a moment as if about to say something more but refrained. 'Do you mind seeing if you can manage my heavier pack and I'll swap for yours?'

'Sure.' Hannah shrugged it on. 'A few more pounds than mine but I'll manage. We'll rest often.'

Will tested his foot by walking around and Hannah helped steady him as he pulled on her lighter pack.

'Thanks. You're a trooper. Let's move on.'

The morning's downhill hiking was slower

although easier than the previous day's gentle steady climb. They stopped often to rest on boulders or logs near the trail and made the picnic area for a late lunch break. Under Will's guidance, Hannah took over the camp fire, boiled the billy and prepared a basic snack. She massaged his leg and rewound and tightened his bandage.

The afternoon's hike was a repeat of the morning, only more tedious, but despite frequent rests and Will's obviously painful limping, they made it back to the carpark well before dusk, giving them plenty of time still to drive through the winding hills back to Tingara by dark.

After they unloaded their packs and stowed them in the boot, Will leant back against the vehicle.

'This car is automatic for which the driver needs their right foot.'

Realisation began to dawn on Hannah. Before he even announced it, she knew what he was about to say.

'I know you've been avoiding it Hannah but you'll have to drive this time. No choice I'm afraid. If it was a straight road I could probably manage but I'd rather not risk our lives on hills,' he said wryly, watching her closely.

Could it be worse? Hannah broke into a cold sweat. 'Bollocks,' she muttered.

'You have an international licence?'

She nodded. The drive from Melbourne on the night of her arrival had been a terrifying nightmare during which she had gripped the wheel until her hands ached and crawled along below the speed limit hugging the left hand white line, sadly dragging out the journey longer than necessary as a result. Every few miles regretting her decision and muttering to herself that she should never have started. She should have stretched out on an airport terminal bench and tried to sleep until the morning train. She would definitely be leaving Ginny's BMW at St. Anne's and taking the XPT back down to the city in plenty of time for her homebound flight in a few weeks.

'Hannah?'

She focused. 'Yes?'

Will voiced her thoughts as if he had just read them. 'You okay to drive?'

'No.'

Worse then embarrassing to watch surprise cross his face. 'But you drove up from Melbourne.'

'Yes I did. Against my better judgement.'

In terror but she would never admit it. And hadn't driven since. Nor expected to. She had deliberately walked or cycled everywhere. For a reason. But not today. Today was an exception. Needs must.

'My driving might be as slow as walking.' She tried to make light of the situation, hiding her inner fear with humour.

'That's okay.' He straightened and rested his hands gently on her shoulders. 'I know the roads are unfamiliar but Ginny's car practically drives itself. You'll be fine.'

He was saying all the right things, boosting her confidence and reassuring. But she still had to drive. She cursed her weakness and this ridiculous fear yet again.

'You'll be fine,' he repeated, following his words with a kiss and warm hug.

'I'm being foolish. Sorry.'

'Take it as slow as you like. Should only be an hour or so.'

Although encouraging, Hannah could see Will was clearly puzzled by her reluctance over a perfectly normal everyday practise. She crossed her fingers and prayed he didn't ask questions.

To boost her morale she told herself that this time it was broad daylight. Well, mostly. And Will was beside her and this time she wasn't alone in the dark. Wasn't overcoming fear simply a matter of facing it?

Hannah helped Will into the passenger seat then climbed in behind the wheel, showing a confidence she didn't feel. She started up the engine and moved from the car park onto the road. Will gave casual navigational instructions, warning her gently ahead of time, keeping her informed and alert.

Once they left the smaller and winding mountain roads to join the main flat road leading across open country to Tingara and civilisation, through concentrated and deep breathing, Hannah felt more comfortable and in control.

She pulled into Will's driveway and turned off the engine.

'Well done,' he beamed, questions lurking behind his steady gaze.

Hannah's returning glance begged him not to ask. Thankfully he kept his own counsel and she helped him unload and carry the packs indoors.

'You okay to drive back down the Lane?' he teased after kissing her.

'I'll just have to manage, won't I?'

'Yes you will.'

His remark could have been taken as advice or support but it was certainly edged with challenge.

'See you tomorrow?'

She nodded. 'I'll come by and see how your foot feels. Should you get it checked out at the hospital?'

'No, just a simple sprain that needs rest for a few days.'

'Thank you for the hike and camp out. Sorry it ended badly for you.'

He chuckled. 'I'll survive.'

They took their time over saying goodbye and parted, Will watching her back out and drive off.

Maybe she could take the BMW out for a drive on her own. On familiar streets around town. She had walked every inch of them and knew her way. Practice. Face this wretched unreasonable fear, Hannah thought with determination. So she could more easily resume driving again in England. Alma might appreciate a drive around the district, too.

She just needed to believe in herself. Build courage and set her mind to the task. Probably time she invested in regular meditation again. She only practised occasionally but found it a relaxing tonic.

In the following days, Hannah jogged down to Wills, fussing and helping where she could. Chatting by the fire with his foot propped up, Hannah making cups of his green tea and snacks. They actually made love again but just the once since it proved awkward and they agreed to abstain a few days more.

To her surprise, Hannah heard briefly from Chelsea. As she suspected, apparently both she and Victoria being fully absorbed in their new boyfriends which took all their free time.

'Vic's heading off on holiday with Mr. Minted. Again,' Chelsea emailed. 'Honestly the man's life is one long holiday. I always get a strange feeling when she goes and worry she might not return.'

Hannah frowned over her youngest sister's concern. Chelsea often complained but never worried about anything or anyone. Unusual. But in the next sentence she raved about her latest flame. Clearly her lover from the unsubtle hints she dropped. Sounded like her whole life revolved around him now because Chelsea actually apologised for her lack of contact. A nice change for her to be so thoughtful. The new man must be having a positive effect.

That night, after being with Will all day, although he was now reasonably mobile again, and answering Chelsea's email with a long reply of her own, cautiously mentioning Will as a friend but giving no details, Hannah slumped into bed, Fluffy across her feet as usual, pleasantly tired.

It felt like she had just fallen asleep when she was woken again by noises. Waking and sitting up, clutching the doona tightly about her, she realised it was coming from downstairs. She listened again. No, outside?

Someone was trespassing in St. Anne's or trying to break in!

Her first thought was to phone Will but she hesitated. She didn't want to risk fresh damage to his foot now it was almost healed by having him traipse down here in the dark. Possibly in false alarm. She would investigate first.

With no weapon to hand, Hannah dragged on her warm robe and pushed her feet into slippers. Using the light from her mobile phone she gingerly peered over the mezzanine balcony.

Maybe she should snap on all the lights. Scare them away.

The front door lock rattled. Hannah heard it creak open, saw faint light issue inside then suddenly all the downstairs lights were switched on. A terrified Fluffy who had leapt downstairs ahead of Hannah, yowled as the intruder trod on her tail.

'Shit! What the hell-?'

A female voice. Sounded familiar. Hannah thought she recognised it. But it couldn't be!

'Ginny?' Hannah's bleary eyes focused.

Not a hair out of place on the woman nor a crease in her clothes and she would have travelled at least one full day from England and many hours up from Melbourne. In the middle of the night?

'Did I wake you? I tried to be quiet.'

Chapter 14

Quiet? Was she kidding? With all that stumbling racket?

Ginny pointed to Fluffy. 'How the hell did that bloody animal get in here?'

'She's a stray.'

'Get it out!'

Hannah quickly combed fingers through her hair in a useless attempt to appear respectable in pyjamas in the middle of the night. She glanced at the bedside clock. 3 a.m?

Her mind whirled as she trotted downstairs and scooped up the terrified cat, slowly edging toward the porch, well remembering Ginny's ban of cats in the house.

'Sorry,' Hannah said, ignoring the feline eyes pleading with her to stay indoors and the mews of complaint as she set Fluffy outside and closed the door, abandoning her to the cold winter night.

Hannah stared at Ginny's two huge suitcases sitting just inside the door. What had she missed? Why was her fellow house-swapper back? Did she get her dates wrong? No, that would never happen. She was too organised for that.

Ginny spread her arms wide, smiling. 'I'm back.'

'So I see.' Hannah tried to project charity over her surprise.

'My circumstances changed.'

'I must have missed your email or text then.' Hannah frowned. 'Or a call?' She had been so preoccupied with Will in recent days it was possible.

Ginny waved away her concern. 'Oh honey, I simply didn't have time for anything like that.'

'It would only have taken a few moments.'

'It all happened so fast. Not my fault.'

Well it certainly wasn't Hannah's. 'I would have appreciated some warning if only out of common courtesy.'

'Like I said, darling, no time.'

Okay if that was how she intended playing it, the gloves were off. She would not be spoken to like an idiot. 'I'm not your darling,' Hannah said firmly.

'No need to be rude. I realise this is a surprise.'

Hannah scoffed. 'It's a little more than that. I'd call it disloyalty to our agreement. By rights, you *should* have let me know. I would have if the circumstances were reversed.'

What happened now? She could hardly share a bed with Ginny. In a moment of enlightenment and panic, Hannah realised Ginny would never back off. This was her home, after all, making Hannah homeless and needing to return to England ASAP.

'I understand this is sticky for you,' Ginny crooned, as if this upheaval was entirely someone else's fault, 'because there is only one bed and it's mine. You can't possibly stay, of course, but I'm not completely heartless.'

Doubtful, Hannah thought, but waited to hear what the cold bitch had to say anyway.

Ginny reached out and ever so lightly touched her shoulder. 'You can sleep on the sofa tonight but I'll definitely need you out in the morning.'

As Ginny gushed, Hannah stood speechless.

'Oh and you'll need to change the sheets for me and remake the bed as soon as possible. While I shower. I'm exhausted.' As she swaggered upstairs, she turned back and over her shoulder said, 'Don't worry about my suitcases. You can bring them up in the morning. I sleep naked anyway.'

In your dreams, Hannah thought, as she crept upstairs, not to do Ginny's bidding but grab a change of clothes for the morning along with a spare blanket and pillow from the linen cupboard before returning downstairs.

When all was quiet above and the lights turned out, Ginny having apparently fallen instantly asleep, Hannah crept back out to the porch, rescued Fluffy, whispering an apology and cuddling his damp fur against her for comfort. She turned up the fire, grabbed the crocheted rug, spread it over the blanket and settled down to try and sleep.

Her head was in turmoil thinking of all she must organise first thing tomorrow. Contact Will and Alma. There she stopped. God. Will. How could she leave him? She wasn't ready to say goodbye. They had only just begun. She wanted to spend so much more time with him here.

Being realistic though, she must book the XPT train from Albury back down to Melbourne and the earliest return flight possible to London. There was a wait of two days before she could leave on an international flight so at least she still had 48 hours still in Australia, her holiday thrown into chaos. She turned on her iPad and made the bookings.

All the thinking and planning kept her awake. She rose, wrapped the crocheted rug about her shoulders and wandered over to the window. A pale shaft of light seeped in at the sides of the drapes. She drew one half aside and looked out onto quiet Gum Tree Lane, barely lit by its infrequent street lights. Will would be sleeping. Hannah checked the antique clock up on the kitchen wall in the altar recess. Actually he might be painting. He had set up his easel in the sunroom again in recent days.

She was thinking of him. Was he thinking of

her? She was so tempted to jog down to his house, bang on the door and dump all her woes on him. He was an awesome listener. Well, pretty much awesome generally. He would happily interrupt his work, make her a huge mug of green tea and settle down to listen.

She started to smile at the thought of him until the weight of her current unexpected predicament sank in. Then suddenly her smile wobbled and tears pooled in her eyes, eventually overflowing to slide down her cheeks. Above everything, she would be desolate without Will. As casual and messy as he was, she adored him. Not a new revelation. She had suspected her true feelings for some time. As much as Will openly showed his attraction and affections for her, Hannah held back. For safety. Because her holiday in Australia was short. Like, the day after tomorrow. With Ginny's reappearance, time had now run out.

Weeks before she expected to, she was forced to think of England again, returning home to her old life, and speed up her future plans to fast forward. What had seemed important before she left, she now questioned. Her work with the Oxford firm had grown stale and the thought of returning to that empty family home left her feeling cold. Unless drastic and immediate changes were made, her existence would continue as before.

What to do? Loads of ideas already charged

around her brain. She would start all over again. Somewhere.

Fluffy brushed against her ankles and she picked him up. 'Are you lonely, too?'

Hannah padded back to the sofa, plonked the cat on the other end then dragged the blanket and rug back over her again. Fluffy changed position, walking over her until he settled in the curve of her body and to the sound of his contented rumbling purr, she drifted into sleep.

Hannah woke to daylight flooding in through the stained glass windows. She frowned at a deep grating sound and at first thought it was the cat. Until she realised it came from the mezzanine. Ginny was snoring!

Plunged back into the reality of her situation with the morning, Hannah was thankful for at least a few hours sleep and made herself a coffee. She couldn't pack with her noisy landlady still asleep upstairs so she picked up her mobile and stared at it for a while, gathering courage to make the first call. To Will.

No. She couldn't do it on the phone. Knowing him, he would probably jog straight down here anyway and that would disturb Ginny. She would have to face him in person. What a dreadful gut wrenching thought. And she would have to repeat the process to Alma across the street, and Emma and Mal, since they had become such lovely friends through Will.

Hannah lingered unnecessarily over her

coffee, slowly pulled on layers of warm clothes and trudged in the chill early morning winter air down to Will's house.

He staggered to the back French doors in trackies and his trademark bare feet. His long ruffled hair softly brushed his shoulders. He smiled at the sight of her. Crumbs, he was gorgeous. And he was hers, sort of. But not for long. Hannah's heart ached for him with affection but also with pain for why she was here. To say goodbye. One of the hardest things in her life she had ever had to do. She was more than attached or attracted. She was in love.

Will opened the door and greeted her with a husky, 'I don't mind being woken up at this sinful hour of the day if it's you.'

'Oh, just make it harder,' Hannah twisted with misery.

He frowned. 'What is it?' reaching for her and drawing her inside to not only the warmth of this lovely sunny room but also the security of his arms. When he hugged her, she broke down and blurted out her dilemma.

Straightening her away from him at arm's length when she finished, he blasted, 'What! We'll go and sort this out right now.'

'She's sleeping.'

He brushed the tears rolling down her cheeks with his thumbs. 'Then we'll wake her up.'

'She won't be impressed.'

'Tough.'

Wow. In all her time here, Hannah had only seen Will display barely controlled anger once before at the city gallery when his parents arrived. He was usually so pacific. From his determined jerky movements and set face, she suspected he was about to erupt.

'It won't do any good. She's back. It's her home.' Hannah protested as he pulled on boots and a padded windbreaker jacket.

'Don't care. This is so wrong.'

'Will.' She caught his arm as they marched down his driveway. 'I just came to say goodbye.' He stopped and stared at her in puzzled disbelief clearly not comprehending what she had said. 'I have no choice,' she added in a small voice, as devastated as he at this sudden new truth between them. 'She told me to get out this morning.'

'We'll see.' He slid an arm about her waist and they walked in silence back up the slight rise in the Lane to St. Anne's.

If anyone saw them – Alma being most likely – they might logically think she had just spent the night under his roof and he was walking her home. But their loving had happened in a far more romantic place.

Will opened the porch door and indicated for her to go in. Once inside, Fluffy scampered over to Hannah.

Will yelled upstairs, 'Ginny?' He repeated his loud demand a few times climbing halfway up the stairs before a gorgeously tumbled Ginny peered over the railing.

'Will, darling.' Her face lit up into a superior smile and her demeanour turned sultry. 'Couldn't keep away, as usual, hmm?'

Will scowled, bewildered. 'Make yourself decent and get down here. We need to talk.'

Ginny pouted and disappeared, returning moments later to descend the stairs wrapped in a slinky black and gold robe. She pointed to an errant Fluffy again and snapped, 'What is that thing doing back in here?' her sweetness gone.

Hannah cringed and opened her mouth to explain when Will scooped up the cat and said easily, 'She must have ducked in when I opened the door.'

He didn't cast her out but instead gently held and stroked her in his arms. 'I have her. She's fine.' Will immediately confronted her. 'What are you doing back?'

'That's no welcome. Aren't you pleased to see me?'

Will glared at her. 'Why?'

'I'm back here to work, of course.'

'Before your three months is up? Without letting Hannah know?'

'Oh, it was all rather rushed.' She waved an arm in the air then turned toward the kitchen. 'Do I smell coffee?'

'Ginny!'

She pressed a hand to her forehead. 'Darling,

I'm still exhausted. Must we do this now?'

'I'm not your darling, Ginny, and never have been. How about the truth, hmm? This place is only your occasional escape. Why aren't you in Melbourne?'

Ginny pushed out a heavy dramatic sigh. 'Because my city penthouse went with my previous job.'

'So you're between jobs then?'

'Not exactly.'

'You don't have one? At all?'

'More or less,' she eventually admitted, squirming with discomfort.

'The great Ginny Bates unemployed!'

'Don't tease, Will. This place is all I have for the moment. But it won't be for long,' she beamed. 'I'll be head hunted any day now. I'll be flooded with offers. It's just a matter of choosing which one.'

'Indeed,' Will said wryly, neither he nor Hannah believing a word she said.

'Excuse me,' Hannah said crisply, 'I'm going upstairs to pack my things.'

'Of course, dear. What are your plans?'

Hannah doubted she cared and couldn't look at Will. She felt gutted. 'I presume I shall fly back home.'

Will was right behind her as she headed for the stairs and caught her hand, winding his fingers through hers. 'Actually, since you've evicted her without notice and until she decides,

Hannah will be staying with me,' Will said softly to Ginny but for Hannah's benefit alone, raising his eyebrows in question.

This was news. Hannah gasped with emotion and gratitude in the face of Will's loaded gaze. He was serious! Or was it just a joke against Ginny? She best play along. In any event, just because she could and because he had asked her and because it would be a well-deserved slap in the face for their haughty audience of one, Hannah closed the space between herself and Will, and pressed up against him.

It was only natural their lips would meet, after all every part of them belonged to each other. The kiss deepened and for a long involved moment, they became lost to all around them.

Hannah grew vaguely aware of her surroundings again when Ginny cleared her throat. 'If you two don't mind,' she bellowed. 'I need you out and packed Hannah. I want my house back.'

'Absolutely.' Hannah began climbing the stairs. As Will followed, she said over her shoulder, 'It's all right. I can manage.'

'I'm impatient to get you into my bed...um, house,' he corrected chuckling.

Hannah gaped and blushed with heat at Will's deliberate suggestive mistake. He was very cheeky this morning. Clearly his foot was better. Before she reached the top stair, he patted her bottom and once in the bedroom, starting pulling her clothes from the dresser and closet, tossing them wildly onto the bed.

'Will! What's your hurry?' she whispered.

'What do you think?'

'Don't just throw everything around. I need to fold everything neatly as I pack so nothing's creased.'

'Doesn't matter,' he drawled. 'You'll be unpacking again straight away. They won't have time to get crushed. Besides,' he grinned, 'for what I have in mind, you won't need any clothes at all.'

'William Bennett!' Hannah laughed with delight.

Chapter 15

So Hannah, dragging all of her belongings behind in her untidy Will-packed rolling suitcase, and the man of the moment clutching Fluffy, all headed for his place down the Lane.

Hannah thought she saw Alma's curtains twitch. They both glanced in that direction.

'I must go and visit her later.'

'It will be killing her not knowing what's going on,' Will grinned.

Hannah turned around as he followed. If ever there was an adorable sight. The man she loved – and the thought was like a dart of excitement through her body – looking scrummy and lovable, grinning broadly and cuddling the cat.

Hannah's heart lifted with the fullest feeling of happiness she had ever known. The only lurking cloud over it all was *the future.*

'Is Callie territorial?' she asked.

'Soon find out.'

'Will you keep her when I'm gone?'

Will scowled. 'We need to have a conversation about that.'

Exactly what Hannah feared but knew she

must face. She wanted all her issues decided soon.

With her gear unceremoniously dumped in his bedroom and Hannah still reeling from the unexpected upheaval of last night and this morning, she and Will stood and stared at each other in the kitchen.

'What now?' she asked, hands planted on her hips, lost.

'A quiet chat?' he suggested.

Hannah took a deep calming breath. 'If it comes with a big fat mug of tea, sure.'

Will brewed a pot of green, set it on a tray on the sunroom table and drew her down beside him on the sofa, Fluffy and Callie stepping around each other getting acquainted nearby.

'You know how I feel about you, Hannah?' She nodded. 'And that I wouldn't deliberately do anything to hurt you in any way?'

'Of course.' She knew where this was leading.

Not wasting a moment, forthright Will came straight out with it. 'You have your licence but you don't like to drive. Why not?'

Even expecting it, Hannah was still shocked by his blunt question because it meant the reason and her reality must now be faced. She *must* tell someone and fate, it seemed, has sent her all the way to Australia for precisely this purpose to confide in this man who she loved and trusted completely.

'It's just a silly fear I have really,' she stalled.

'Doesn't sound insignificant to me. What triggered it off?'

Oh God. The time was here to tell him. Confess her fear and the niggling guilt behind it all. Wary at laying herself open to ridicule and being considered weak but believing in Will's natural compassion and hoping he could understand, Hannah crossed her fingers so tight they hurt and began.

'My parents' deaths.'

'In what way?'

Hannah looked down at her restless hands as she spoke, not daring to look at Will. Even thinking about it, forcing herself to not only remember but voice it, made her stomach churn. Time and distance had not made the memories fade.

'On the day they died a whole string of events came into play. It was going to be a long day for my parents. I knew they would be tired by evening so that's why I planned to drive. We all rose early to leave home by 7.30. I drove the 20 minutes from our village to Moreton-in-Marsh railway station where we all took the 8.11 train into Oxford, leaving the car parked all day.

'My mother had a medical appointment at a hospital, some sort of scan or x-ray or day procedure.' Hannah frowned. 'They never did make it clear at the time but we all found out later. Anyway, from the station, we all caught a taxi to the hospital where my parents left and I went into my office for the day. We had parted, I believed, on the understanding that I would meet them at the hospital about 5 pm in a taxi for the station to get the 5.25 home. To this day, I still wonder if I didn't make it clear enough for them.'

Hannah almost choked on her next admission. 'As always, I was frantic at work and left a few minutes later than I would have liked. Then the taxi was held up in traffic and I was definitely running late.' She paused. 'My parents didn't have a mobile so I rang the hospital and left a message. Maybe they misunderstood and thought they had to make their own way home or were just anxious to get home after the hospital. We'll never know why they didn't wait. When I arrived, the nurses told me they seemed in a hurry and had already left.

'They weren't at the station waiting for me when I got there, so I presumed they had taken the earlier train as planned. I took the next one an hour later. I waited and paced and worried. Mother's treatment apparently meant mild sedation so father drove home the 20 minutes from the train. His eyesight was poor. He didn't drive at all in the village. No need really. They could walk everywhere. But he never drove at night anymore and only did the weekly drive and shop to Broadway.

'The roads home are quiet narrow country lanes but from October to March, it's dark by five so, on the evening of the accident, being early spring, by the time my parents were on the road around six they would have been travelling at night. Not to mention driving along shady narrow lanes edged closely with trees and shrubs. Single lane roads, no lines. Three miles from home they needed to cross a busy intersection.'

Hannah shared a glance of understanding with Will. He would guess where this was going. 'Maybe the glare of headlights from other traffic confused father or he was surprised by suddenly coming out from a shady narrow line onto the crossing and headlights. For whatever reason that we'll never know, but most likely preoccupied and devastated by the day's events and bad news, father obviously misjudged the approach or didn't expect it so soon, and didn't slow down. He was familiar with our local area but didn't drive it much.'

At this point, Will wrapped an arm around her shoulder and squeezed her hand. Hannah almost cracked but swallowed hard and forced herself to continue.

'Anyway the worst happened, and a lorry crashed into the side of them, killing father instantly. Mother died a few days later,' Hannah said with soft sadness. 'The lorry driver reported that he saw the car come out from the side road and cross in front of him giving him no time to brake. He only noticed two people in the car, a male driver and a passenger, and that the driver was focused strictly on the road in front of him. He didn't look in either direction, just straight ahead.

'We all learnt later from the medical staff that our parents were tired and confused when they left the hospital after a stressful day of travelling and probably worried about mother's tests. They received bad news that she was terminally ill and we all believe it shook them up and they just wanted to get home. Father would have been distraught at the thought of losing his life time spouse. Our parents did everything together and were a devoted couple.

'It's a horrid thought but the accident could have been fate's ironic blessing that they both died together.'

Will released a heavy sigh. 'So you've been living with this tragedy the past year?'

Hannah nodded, feeling sick and bleak reliving it all. 'From the station I phoned our neighbour and asked her to check on my parents. Make sure they were home safe. Ever since missing the connection with them in Oxford I had this dreadful feeling.' Hannah shook her head. 'I waited on the phone while she checked but our cottage was in darkness and no car in the garage. I grabbed a taxi and we came across the accident scene.' Hannah raised a hand to her mouth, tears welling in her eyes. 'They nearly made it. Only three more miles. If I hadn't been running late and met them as planned, the crash would never have happened.'

She looked at Will, filled with guilt and agony. 'I'm responsible for my parents' deaths.'

'No, Hannah. Don't-'

'I killed them Will.'

At that point, overwhelmed by remembering the awful accident scene and recalling her feelings and memories, Hannah finally broke down and shook with weeping. Sobbing against Will, he caressed her, uttered soothing words, pressed warm kisses to her forehead, murmured into her hair, held her tight and rode out the emotional storm while she was safely folded in his arms.

'You've never told anyone else all this, have you?' Will said gently as Hannah settled and he brushed aside the tears from her cheeks with his thumbs.

She shook her head. 'Not how I feel responsible, no.'

'What was the official finding?'

'The inquest? Accidental death.'

'You can't accept that, too?'

'A nagging guilt still haunts me. I know it's an illogical sense of responsibility. All the *what ifs?* But life is fate. I get that.'

'It's not always easy to move on,' Will murmured. 'Takes determination and courage for that first step.'

Hannah tilted up her face to study him as he

spoke and watched shadows cross his face. Was he referring to his own life and differences with his parents?

'Seems we both need to try and completely dump our pasts,' Hannah noted, sitting up straight again. 'You know, my sisters have never said anything but I know they think it's my fault.'

'Have they said so?'

'No but I can see it in their eyes.'

'Have you ever spoken to them about it?'

'Of course not.'

'Then how do you know? Ask them.'

'I'm too afraid. At the time, they questioned me about why I was late and why did I let them drive home alone in the dark? I grew defensive and that started a kind of love-hate sisterhood ever since.'

Will groaned. 'They're making you feel guilty?'

'Not intentionally but maybe only Chelsea and Victoria really. Possibly it's just my perception, too, feeling guilty as I do. Heather seems to have accepted everything. The accident was so sudden, it hit the younger ones hardest.'

'It affected you all,' Will pointed out.

Hannah knew there was much unspoken baggage in her family but had felt too overwhelmed in the past to address it and so the vicious circle of her unhappy existence continued.

'You won't have closure until you speak to your sisters about how you feel and clear the air. You'll ruin your health again and be right back where you started when you first arrived.'

'I'll think about it.'

Will put a finger beneath her chin, forcing her to face him. 'Avoiding talking to your sisters won't solve all this.'

'I know,' Hannah moaned. 'And they all wanted to keep the family home. Voted me to stay in residence. Keeping a link with the past, I guess,' she shrugged, shuddering with the remnants of emotion. 'I do all the upkeep and gardening but none of my sisters contribute toward the expense and maintenance of such an historical cottage.'

'Sneaky of them,' Will said wryly.

'Not sure it's intentional. It's a beautiful house and I do love it. It's been our family home but it's so much work when I'm commuting full time into Oxford. I never have time for anything else. The catalyst before I came was the nightmares. I can't live in the house when I return,' she admitted in a small voice. 'Its agony living with so many memories and just making me feel worse.'

'So you worked yourself hard to avoid having to make a decision or stop and think, right?' Will suggested.

'I've grown to hate the place I used to love. I won't argue with my sisters. When I get back,

I'm moving out and it simply must be sold.'

'Good for you. One step at a time. And now, my beautiful woman,' he rose and pulled her up beside him. 'You've had an emotional 24 hours and you need rest.'

And then, because it was days since they had first made love, with Hannah's emotions now raw from her confessions, leaving her vulnerable, and it was clear from Will's intense gaze and her own responding need that they both wished for the same thing, they kissed and stumbled all the way to his room.

Now this, Hannah thought, was what she would call a holiday. Who knew she would be changing houses before it was over? And finally be able to confess the deep guilt and fears of the past year.

She wanted to give herself so badly to this man for all he had done to help her these past months but also for simply being Will. Slight hiccup. Where would this passion lead? No. She mustn't overthink everything. In her heart she knew she and Will together were so much more than a holiday romance. Her feelings and their chemistry were deep and real.

So she ignored her unpacked bags on the floor and fell into Will's arms and his huge soft bed.

'I hope this means you're going to take advantage of me,' Hannah whispered.

Will chuckled and she allowed herself to be fully loved.

Afterwards, she fell asleep, waking to find Will sitting cross legged at the other end of the bed, sketching. He wore only boxer shorts leaving his muscled chest bare.

When she stirred, he looked up and smiled. Hannah's heart curled with love as he slowly flipped around the artist's pad in his hands to reveal a charcoal drawing of Hannah in repose, half naked with the sheet partly drawn up over her.

Seeing it, feeling utterly loved and mellow and unthreatened by his answer, she asked him bravely, 'Did you ever sleep with Ginny?' When he winced, Hannah raised a hand. 'Not judging. Just asking.'

He laid down his sketch pad. 'Just the once. It was a weak moment that I'll always regret. I was ashamed of myself afterwards because I knew what she was like but I've never loved her.'

'She's a powerful woman. Lots of seductive energy.'

'Only to get what she wants. It's a very cold heart beating in her chest.'

'I've only had one other lover,' she admitted softly. 'After this morning, I've realised he was really rather poor. You tick every, single, box.'

She rose from the sheets, crawled toward him and sat in his lap. Will took control, again, until she knew in her heart that *this* was right and she never wanted to be loved by anyone else.

Afterwards, Will asked, 'What's next for you,

then?'

'I have a few weeks left of my holidays. I've booked my return flight and leave in two days.'

'Do you want to?'

'Pardon?'

'Leave.'

'Not really, I guess,' she grinned, 'but I must.'

'Stay on here with me?' he invited softly.

Hannah wavered, considering his offer. 'I'm sorry, Will. I need to do one last thing. I can't.'

'You mean you won't. Sure you're still not being ruled by the past and your family?'

'No. I mean I really can't. I need to go back and sell the house.'

'Your sisters can do it, can't they? Only one person needs to sign all the paperwork and the others can give permission for her to do it.'

'Of course. I should have realised that.'

When she hesitated, Will drawled, 'Stay with me. At least for the rest of your holidays. You were intending to anyway until Ginny returned, right?'

Hannah chuckled. 'You're making this impossible. Won't you be busy painting or organising that subdivision with Mal or something? Instead of playing host to a tourist.'

'Oh, I think you're a little more than that now.' Will grinned then grew serious again. 'Life's a moving object, Hannah. I live in Tingara but, for you, right now, I'm entirely flexible.'

Hannah knew exactly how flexible Will

Bennett was. 'You would do that for me?' She grew excited. 'All right. I'll phone Heather.' She glanced at the clock. 'Crumbs. It's four in the morning in England. I'll wait for a few hours. Little Andy usually wakes her up early. Seven should work.'

Hannah could barely contain her happiness. Will wanted her to stay. Maybe her life was finally falling into place after all.

Since they were both starving, Will whipped up a stir fry in the wok that they forked up from bowls in their laps sitting together in their favourite place – the sunroom sofa. Even after a few hours together, Callie and Fluffy were now warily tolerant of each other.

Later, Will set out his art supplies again and began drafting the outline of a fresh work on his easel. Meanwhile, Hannah kept the wood fire stoked and the artist plied with mugs of green tea.

Mid-afternoon, Alma appeared at the French doors, her brow wrinkled in concern.

Hannah and Will glanced at each other. 'She's seen Ginny.'

Will welcomed her inside and while he took a break from sketching, they explained the happenings of the last twenty four hours.

'Well I never,' Alma said. 'All very unexpected and you don't have to leave so soon after all,' she beamed at Hannah, patting her hand. Then in the same breath, she announced, 'I have news of my own. I wrote to my oldest son Martin and explained everything you found out about his father. I thought it would be easier for him to digest than a telephone call.'

'And?'

'He phoned me two nights ago but you two were up in the mountains hiking so I couldn't tell you. I was going across to St. Anne's this morning when I saw Ginny drive off in her car.' Her face turned ashen. 'I thought you'd already left, dear, without saying goodbye.'

'I would never do that,' Hannah reassured her swiftly. 'Go on.'

Tears glinted in Alma's eyes. 'Anthony and Sam don't really remember their father. Anthony only had vague images and Sam not at all. So they've never felt the need to ask after Bernie and, of course, I never spoke of him,' Alma said with regret, then brightened. 'But Martin remembers his Dad. He said he couldn't face me without feeling guilty because he was too young and small and afraid of defending me against his father when he grew rough. He knew he was the oldest and should have done something to protect me but his father was too strong. Imagine that!'

Alma sniffed, producing a handkerchief from her cardigan pocket and dabbing her eyes. 'That poor boy. All these years feeling so bad because he didn't help me. It's opened a door in our family, Hannah. What you've done. And do you know what Martin's doing now? Applying for Bernie's death certificate and we're flying to Queensland. I've never been on a plane,' she giggled like a girl. 'Brisbane first apparently then a regional flight to Toowoomba and Cunnamulla.'

'Alma, that's brilliant.'

'We're staying at a small boutique hotel for a few days while we visit Bernie's grave and the bank to see what's in that safe deposit box. I'm that excited I can hardly sleep.'

'When are you going?' Will asked.

'Next weekend.'

'It will be hot up there,' he said. 'Pack light and take a sunhat.'

'Will you be gone when I get back?' Alma asked Hannah.

She felt Will's eyes on her. 'Probably. I have your address and phone number. I'll keep in touch. Promise.'

'That would be wonderful, dear. You've a lovely girl. Pity you're returning to England.' She glanced between Hannah and Will. 'I wish my daughters-in-law were more approachable. Martin says after our Queensland trip, he'll bring his wife and the grandchildren up for a visit.'

'It's a new beginning for you, Alma,' Hannah said. She knew all about those although the details in her own life were still undecided.

They all hugged and Alma left. When night

set in, Hannah constantly checked the time on her phone, anxious for seven o'clock.

'Go on,' Will bustled her out of the kitchen. 'Make the call while I get dinner.'

Hannah was wired with anticipation as she listened to Heather's number dialling.

Her sister had barely answered before Hannah gushed, 'Hi, Heather, it's Hannah. From Australia.'

But instead of an excited return greeting, Heather blasted, 'Thank heavens you called.'

From her sister's anxious voice, Hannah immediately sensed something wrong. 'What's the matter?'

'Our bloody sisters, that's what! Both of them. Has Chelsea not been in touch?'

'Only a brief email about ten days ago saying she was busy with work and her new boyfriend and that Victoria's off on holiday somewhere. Again.'

'Her rich old Greek sugar daddy demanded she go with him on his yacht to Monte Carlo. Wouldn't take no for an answer apparently. Sounds like he's become a bully. Vic said she's intimidated by him and felt it was smarter not to refuse. He turns on the charm to keep her with him and she's afraid to leave. He promises her the world to get his own way. You know how materialistic our sister is,' Heather ended dryly.

All Hannah's good news scattered in her brain as Heather talked, and she scrambled to think of a way out for Vic. 'Can't Chelsea go and rescue her? They move in the same circles. Threaten him with the police or something?'

'No. The chap has body guards that trail them everywhere and watches Vic's every move.' Heather paused at length before adding, 'Besides, Chelsea has a problem of her own.'

Hannah hated to ask. As it happened, she didn't have to. Heather plunged on.

'Hannah, Chelsea's pregnant.'

She stopped pacing the sunroom and sank onto the sofa. 'What!'

'Hannah, it's all a mess over here. You have to come home and help sort it out.'

Hannah's bubble of happiness burst. She had been about to change her travel booking to stay in Australia another two weeks, after rapidly changing it the other night, believing she had no other option. Until Will's offer. Now it seemed she would need that return flight in two days after all.

When she glanced across at Will in the kitchen, he looked up and smiled.

Hannah's heart broke.

Chapter 16

Feeling frustrated and powerless in the aftermath of Heather's phone conversation, Hannah sighed with resignation over the intervention of fate once more in her life, and explained to Will the latest eruption of events back home.

He leaned back against the kitchen counter, arms folded, unapproachable, looking thunderous. He knew.

'You're leaving.' She nodded. 'You're still doing it. Living for your sisters, jumping as soon as they snap their fingers. When are you going to wake up and stop being a doormat for them all? Family loyalty is all well and good up to a point but they're still controlling you.'

Anxious and tired, Hannah said hotly, 'What would you know about it? Your family is hardly a role model so what right do you have to make such a judgement? You hardly have the best experience in that area, do you? At least our family talks!'

Will stared at her in astonishment.

'They're my sisters, Will. My family. They're

all I have. Even halfway around the world and being pestered by them, I will always be there for them, okay? You might not talk to them or see them but at least you still have parents. You should be grateful for that.'

She wanted to believe Will's criticism was uttered out of selfishness, wanting her to stay longer. Her wish, too.

'It's a bit late to help Chelsea,' she said wryly, then frowned, 'but Victoria's situation sounds unhealthy and threatening.'

'Heather's closer. Can't she investigate?' Will said carefully when he finally spoke again

'She has a family. Michael can't just leave work to mind the boys. Who knows how long it will take? Besides, a woman alone heading into that predicament is unwise. I'll go with her. Maybe Chelsea can help out with her nephews. It will be good practice for her own future by the sound of it.'

'You've already decided.'

'It's my choice to make,' she challenged.

'It still sounds like you're not in control of your own life. Yet,' Will muttered.

'This time, I am. Whether we like it or not, this one's a no-brainer, Will. Victoria could be in danger. At the least, I want to find her, talk to her. Make sure she's all right emotionally and physically. Not being forced to stay against her will.'

'If she wasn't she would be home by now,

surely? She would leave, wouldn't she?'

'Not necessarily. There are many different kinds of manipulation. Victoria tends to let people take advantage. She's been in sticky situations in the past. Sounds like this one's urgent and possibly out of hand.'

'Can't you or Heather phone the local authorities to try and locate Victoria? Check out her circumstances. She may be just fine.'

'True, but I have a really bad feeling about this. I need to go. For my own peace of mind. She's family, Will. Please understand.'

He shrugged. 'Naturally I'd love you to stay longer. And I *do* realise it's somewhat of a family crisis and that the girls are important to you.'

Did she detect a note of envy in his voice? That she readily sprang to her sisters' side when necessary, despite their shortcomings, when Will was unable or unwilling to do the same to restore a relationship with his parents?

She stepped toward him. 'Can we take a break from this discussion and have dinner? It smells amazing.'

Instead of taking her in his arms as she hoped, Will turned away and began serving up their meal. Hannah was disappointed in his mini rejection, as if she hadn't been equally robbed of the same opportunity to share the promising last weeks of her holiday together, too. That he also felt it keenly gave her hope that he might want to keep in touch but when and how remained unspoken, leaving her emotions in turmoil. Maybe the distance thing would prove too much of a deal breaker for them.

An unusually solemn Will asked, 'When's your flight?'

'Tomorrow night. I've booked the afternoon train that gets into the city early evening, leaving me enough time to make the airport and check in a few hours before midnight.'

With only tonight and half a day tomorrow left in Tingara, her holiday was practically over. She longed for Will to make arrangements with her to meet again. Somehow. Somewhere. Keep in touch. Surely he wanted that, too? But he said nothing and, with loads to preoccupy her mind over what lay ahead back home for her sisters, Hannah remained silent.

All he said was, 'I had thought of throwing you a farewell party with our friends.'

'That was a lovely thought. There's no time now, sadly, though, is there?' she said regrettably.

'No. Seems not.'

After their humour and carefree loving of earlier today, this strain was unbearable. They were still parting, only sooner.

'I might use the morning to drop in on Emma and Nick. Say goodbye.'

Will nodded and began clearing their dishes, distracted. Understandable when each had their own thoughts to contemplate.

That night, their loving was subdued and bittersweet, restrained, as if both withheld a part of themselves, unwilling or afraid to release their normal abandon with each other.

The morning proved no less awkward with Hannah fussing and folding clothes, packing carefully, cramming her own knitwear and winter buys into the corners of her case, knowing she would make good use of them in the coming English winter. Just as the damp air and warming fires of the approaching autumn were taking place on the other side of the world, the first enticing signs of spring here in Australia were already on display.

Early golden wattle shimmered on trees and shrubs in gardens and the bush, bringing its usual dun greenery to life. Hannah didn't anticipate another cold snowy season following on from the memorable and joyous one she had experienced in Tingara, but was grateful for everything it had brought into her life.

'I'll be off then,' Hannah said immediately after breakfast.

'You can borrow *Dora*,' Will offered.

'Thanks anyway,' she grinned, never having faced the challenge of driving his classic old vehicle. 'It's a glorious day. I'll take the bike. It will be all yours again, soon.'

Her attempt at lightness fell flat. She cycled up the Lane, past St. Anne's. Ginny's BMW was in the driveway. The woman had been mysteriously invisible since her arrival.

Hannah visited Emma at The Stables first.

'Will was planning a party,' Emma complained in dismay shocked by the news of her sudden departure.

'So he said.'

'He'll miss you.'

'I hope so,' Hannah confessed.

'So, what's the deal between you two?'

'To be honest, Emma, I have absolutely no idea.'

'He adores you.'

She sighed. 'If it's meant to be it will work out.'

'He's not going with you?' Hannah shook her head. 'You'll miss our wedding in the spring,' Emma heaped on yet more sadness, adding to Hannah's anguish and regret.

'I'll be with you in spirit. Send me loads of pictures.'

'I should send you an invitation. Make you come back.'

Hannah laughed and then, with both women holding back tears, they hugged, swapping phone numbers and emails. Emma waved and watched Hannah cycle away toward the edge of town and Stony Creek Way where Nick lived.

No guarantees the man would be home, Hannah knew. He was usually on the road weekdays, keeping his weekend trips to a minimum so he could be with his three boys. So she was delighted to see the gentle giant with his head and shoulders bent over a truck engine.

'Hiya,' she greeted, leaning her bike against the veranda of his lovely big weatherboard house and walking over to him.

Nick smiled and straightened, wiping his greasy hands on a rag. 'Morning.'

Hannah sank her hands into her coat pockets. 'I'm leaving today. Just came to say goodbye.'

She felt uncomfortable beneath Nick's frown. Everyone thought she was staying until the end of the month so, once more, Hannah plunged into explanations.

'Family's important,' Nick said with conviction and understanding, the only one so far not questioning her early leaving. He accepted her reasoning. Perhaps because he had personally experienced a fractured family life, raising his sons alone, trying to be both father and mother to them. According to the Tingara grapevine, his ex-wife was rarely in their lives.

Hannah felt for his sad circumstances. A warm hearted family man like Nick deserved a woman in his life. Someone motherly, Hannah predicted, to take his male brood beneath her wings and shower them with the woman's loving touch she was sure they all missed in their home.

'Can you stay for a cuppa?' Nick offered.

'Sorry. No time.'

He trailed her back to the bike.

'No sign of a new neighbour yet?' Hannah nodded toward the red SOLD sticker slashed across the sale sign on the acreage property next door.

She thought the cottage cute. Neglected and overgrown but with its charms well-hidden she was sure.

'A woman bought it, so Anne Perry says.' He scowled. 'A tree changer maybe. Apparently plans to start up a garden nursery. Apart from Ivy's flower shop, the town sure needs one.'

'It's been wonderful to meet you and your family, Nick. You must be so proud of your handsome boys.'

'When they're behavin',' he chuckled.

When he hesitated to approach her, Hannah stepped forward and stood on tiptoe to give him a hug, almost breaking down at yet another nostalgic goodbye and the painful thought of leaving not only Will but these new friends she had made and grown to care about in such a short space of time. Who were already halfway to becoming like family.

For Hannah, returning to Gum Tree Lane, packing her bag, zipping it up and wheeling it to the sunroom door was a heartbreaking jolt of reality.

Her time was up. She was leaving Tingara.

Unable to eat, she refused lunch but Will insisted on driving her to the Albury station. The tension inside a confined and rattling *Dora* lay heavy on them both.

Parting from Will, she barely held it together. He lifted her case on board, stowed it in the baggage area then returned to the platform for a kiss of such tender pleasure edged with anguish, it was almost Hannah's undoing.

Will remained stoic so she refused to cry. This sudden choice for leaving was made for all the right reasons this time. She would have been gone in two weeks anyway. But Will offered no crumb of hope, nothing to look forward to.

Hannah stared at him wishing he would open his mouth and spit it out that he loved her madly. Which she hoped more than anything else in the world. She adored him and wanted to be with him but only if he asked. She refused to take the initiative and put herself out there and throw herself at any man. If a chap wanted her, he must let her know. Show it by actions. But he just stared right back and said nothing. Infuriatingly calm as you like.

'We'll stay in touch, yeah?'

At last, something to cling to. 'Please.'

He kissed her quickly again before she stepped onto the train. She still felt the remembered touch of Will's lips on hers as she settled into her seat, refusing to look out the window to even wave a casually fake goodbye. She would dissolve if she saw him again and watch him grow smaller as the train slowly pulled away.

He had let her go so easily. Crushing to bear. *Stay in touch?* What did that mean anyway? If she was lucky she may find out one day. Sooner rather than later, she hoped.

Hannah chose the night flight and business class so she could sleep. Because if she slept she wouldn't think of Will. Should she have been more careful with her feelings?

Sleep of course was the ideal and she managed some but basically her homeward flight was miserable. After all, she had just left the man she loved. Messy, gorgeous, frustrating, talented Will Bennett. How big of an idiot did that make her when the future lay so open and uncertain between them?

After an hour layover mid journey, Hannah touched down less than twenty four hours later in London. At least the late summer morning was warmer in England than the Tingara winter she had just left. She hauled her bag along the underground walkway and caught a bus direct to Oxford. By now, operating on autopilot, Hannah forced herself to stay awake.

Heather met her at the bus and her boys kissed and hugged Auntie Hannah who they hadn't seen for a long time before driving home to their village.

'I didn't hear from you much. Figured you would be busy.' Hannah glanced in the rear view mirror at the two chatty boys in the back seat. 'We need to sell the house,' she blurted out what had been playing on her mind.

'This is news. I thought you wanted to keep it?'

'We all did but I can't live there anymore. It tears me apart living with memories of Mum and Dad everywhere. I can't do it anymore, Heather.'

'Really? You never said.'

'My bad,' Hannah admitted, yawning. 'We'll check with the others but it could easily fetch half a million pounds. With each share, we can all move on with our lives.'

'Well I'm not going anywhere,' Heather laughed, 'but with that amount of money Michael and I could pay off our mortgage and own our house. We might take a bang-up family holiday first, though.'

'If the other two are wise, they'll budget, invest in a property, or keep it aside as a nest egg for the future. Where's Chelsea?'

'Waiting at home. She's a mess. Literally. Chucks up all over the place.' Heather grinned. 'I know what *that* feels like.'

Hannah sighed. 'Okay, I'll chat to her. What's the latest on Victoria?'

Heather shook her head. 'That's the problem. We haven't heard from her in weeks and when she did finally answer Chelsea's call, she spoke low as if she was trying to keep her voice down and not be overheard. All we know is that she was off to Monte Carlo with her rich old boyfriend in a yacht with an entourage of minders. Since then she hasn't answered any phone calls or texts. Victoria loves the high life but she usually keeps in touch.'

'Yes, definitely odd. She and Chelsea are top communicators.'

'It's so good to have you back,' Heather said with meaning.

Thrust into the midst of all the family problems again, Hannah wasn't so sure. Suddenly, a pang for missing Will cut through her.

'You look tired,' Heather noted. 'Understandable after the long flight but Chelsea is desperate for a chinwag so I hope you can stay awake long enough to listen.'

'I'll survive.'

'I'll take the boys out into the garden for a while. Give you time alone with her.'

'Thanks.'

When they approached and crossed the fateful intersection before the village where their parents had been killed, Hannah closed her eyes against the tragic memories.

'Hard, isn't it?' Heather said quietly, a catch in her voice.

Hannah opened her eyes and nodded.

And then they were home. Hannah had barely unloaded her suitcase from the car and Heather released the energetic boys into the back garden when Chelsea appeared looking red eyed and miserable. She fell all over her big sister.

Overwhelmed when they weren't even in the cottage yet, exhausted, and hauling her heavy case, Hannah allowed Chelsea to grab her free arm as they walked inside.

'I'm so glad you're home.'

Maybe but only for how she could help, Hannah thought. So far neither sister had been interested enough to ask anything about her Australian holiday. But Hannah had a plan and when her sisters were sorted, she would put it into action.

Chelsea dropped onto the settee and wailed, 'I had plans. I wanted to go to Paris, New York. All the top fashion houses.' She turned weepy pleading eyes on Hannah. 'You'll help me with this baby, won't you?'

'No.'

Chelsea reeled back in surprise to have her sweet cajoling rejected.

'You're an adult making adult choices. Choice number one should have been contraception. You're on your own with this one.'

'But I don't know anything about babies.'

'You'll learn. Heather did. I have my own life to live.'

Chelsea now sat up wide eyed and taking notice.

'So what's the deal with the baby's father? Do you love him?'

'No!' She seemed appalled by the suggestions.

'So, just a fling then.'

'It wasn't like that!'

'Chelsea, all your boyfriends are *like that.* Time to get real. You're going to be a mother. Will the father be around? You should know where you stand financially and with support.'

Chelsea looked embarrassed. 'He left when I told him,' she muttered.

'The weak ones always do. Okay. Single mother then.' Hannah had already mentioned selling the cottage. 'Your share would buy you a small one or two bedroom modest flat in Oxford. And you can take whatever you like from here. Furniture and so on. You can probably borrow baby stuff from Heather. Anyway, I suggest you start looking for your own place. At least it would be a room over your head.' She glanced around the sitting room. 'We won't have this place much longer. If you choose Oxford, Heather is nearby but don't depend on her. She has a family of her own to raise.'

'Everything's changed, Han,' Chelsea moaned.

It sure had. 'You'll be fine. It might be months until the cottage is sold so you can live here.'

'Could I?'

'Now you'll be entitled to a single parent benefit, your council tax will be reduced, you'll have income support and a weekly child benefit.'

Chelsea gaped. 'How do you know all this?'

'My job. Short term you could also borrow my car.'

Chelsea's eyes doubled. 'Won't you need it?'

'I plan on taking a break from work and travelling for a while. Experience the world. Widen my horizons.'

'That's what I wanted to do,' Chelsea sobbed afresh.

'You'll have a chance in the future. We all need to find Victoria first,' Hannah changed the subject as a distraction.

It worked. 'We're that worried about her, Han.'

'Hopefully all will be well and we can all get on with our lives.'

Hannah hoped she made her intentions clear for the future. That her sisters' problems were exactly that. Their problems, not hers. When Heather returned with her rowdy boys, they all sat down with a cup of tea to chat.

Chelsea made sandwiches for lunch.

Hannah was gobsmacked. 'Thank you.'

'Heather made me,' she admitted.

'All the same.'

Was her little sister finally showing even the smallest signs of growing up and being responsible? About time! But the pantry and refrigerator were bare, Hannah had noticed, and made a mental note to go shopping in Broadway before she left for Europe tomorrow to trace

Victoria.

Meanwhile the sisters all agreed to bombard her with texts and phone calls. See if they produced any response. Hannah phoned the Monaco police but hung up and shook her head at the others waiting on her every word.

'Not a lot they can do but they will keep an eye out and ask around. They have my mobile number if anything arises and I'll contact them when we get to Monaco.'

Heather agreed to see a solicitor and a real estate agent to have the cottage valued and its sale underway.

Late afternoon, Heather drove back to Oxford with the boys, planning to return tomorrow to start going through all the house cupboards. Hannah sank back with relief that at least Heather was being helpful and proactive with Chelsea showing signs in the right direction.

That night, Hannah expected to lie awake, brooding over Will but was so exhausted from her flight and the busy day since landing at Heathrow, plunged straight into family happenings, that she fell instantly asleep.

Next morning when she woke and looked around her room, Hannah realised it would be one of the last times she would most likely ever use it. But her deep sense of sadness and nostalgia for their family cottage was tinged with a feeling of freedom and a new start.

Just one more difficult task to perform this

morning, some urgent shopping, then checking for flights to Nice, Monaco's nearest airport. She would hire a car from there and deliberately test her driving aversion. The fact she was even considering that option, Hannah counted as progress.

When Heather arrived from Oxford after breakfast without the boys, Michael having offered to mind them for the day, Hannah announced her intention to visit the cemetery. She apologised for not wanting to participate with her sisters three months ago before going to Australia.

Heather hugged her warmly. 'Well, the holiday seems to have helped. It's fabulous that you can now. Better late than never.'

'Anyone else want to come?'

'Let's all go,' Heather suggested.

Before she left for Australia, Hannah had refused to visit her parents' graves. But this time, with determination, a fresh approach in her mind since confiding in Will and also Heather upon her return, she felt braver.

All three women embraced the summer morning, striding downhill past the cottage row hugging the street, climbing roses scrambling over their golden stone facades to St. Barnabas church and the cemetery set within a low stone walled triangle in the village heart.

Hannah unlatched the wooden gate and the daughters strolled to their parents' gravesite. As

Heather placed the bunch of profuse flowers picked fresh from their garden that morning, Hannah began to murmur a private conversation with her parents.

'Hi Mum and Dad, I'm back. Been to Australia for a few months on the journey of a lifetime really as it happens although I didn't know it before I left. Met some lovely people, one in particular, who helped me confront my grieving over your loss.' She placed a hand over her heart. 'You'll always be in here and I loved you both dearly but I might not visit for a while. I plan to quit my job and travel. Be a free spirit for a time.'

Heather and Chelsea stared at their sister in surprise.

'We all wish you were still here, of course,' she grasped her sisters' hands and squeezed, 'but I've decided to stop blaming myself because you're not. I'm sorry we missed each other on that last day but I know it was fate and not my fault that caused your accident.'

'Oh Hanny, you never said,' Chelsea turned to her and whispered.

'That's what I told her yesterday,' Heather added. 'She's been feeling responsible for a whole year and wretched living in the cottage as well, and never said a thing. Can you imagine?'

'And I loaded you with all my troubles as well,' Chelsea said with genuine regret. 'I do tend to rely on you, don't I? But you're so organised and I don't have mother anymore.'

'Neither do I,' Hannah retorted.

'No, of course not. I'm sorry.'

Hannah had never seen her youngest sister so contrite. Before they left the cemetery, there were lots of tears and hugs and apologies all around so the women were chattering warmly again, arms linked, as they walked uphill back to the cottage.

'Well I need to drive into Broadway for supplies,' Hannah said the moment they returned. 'Chelsea you should come. You won't be eating out much anymore I shouldn't imagine, so you should know how to shop.'

'And cook,' Heather put in.

'You can teach her. I won't be around for a while.'

'How long will you be away?' Chelsea asked cautiously.

'No idea.'

'You *are* coming back?'

'Eventually,' she laughed. 'Come on, let's get food.'

'While you're away I'll make a start on going through cupboards and stuff. We'll need to sort through it all and see what we keep or distribute among us, and what must be sold,' Heather said.

Hannah sighed. 'Yes. Back soon.'

An hour later, Heather greeted her on return with, 'Well, you're a dark horse.'

'Pardon?' She dumped their grocery bags on

the kitchen counter.

'Some chap called to see you while you were out.'

'The estate agent already? Why didn't you talk to him?'

'No. It was a personal visitor for you.'

Hannah frowned. 'Not someone from the Oxford firm because if they want me back, it's not happening.'

Heather shook her head. 'This chap had long hair in a ponytail and shabby clothes.'

Hannah froze. No!

Chapter 17

Hannah tried to get her head around the bombshell Heather had just dropped.

'I thought he had the wrong house except he asked for you.'

Hannah didn't need a name. Keeping her back turned, by now totally distracted from unpacking groceries and trying to sound casual, she asked, 'He didn't wait?'

'I didn't invite him in. He was a stranger.'

'No message?'

'Said he'd be down the pub. Who is he?'

'Um, Will. Someone I met in Australia.'

Hannah checked the clock. Lunch time. Would he wait? Stupid, he had come all this way, surely that meant something. Her heart raced.

'Where are you going?' Heather asked as her sister dashed into the hall to check herself in the mirror.

'Out.'

Her cheeks were far too flushed but nothing to be done. They would be worse by the time she ran downhill to the *Arms*. God, she would have to do.

Heather trailed her to the door and hovered. 'So, this chap has followed you all the way out from Australia? That's so romantic.'

'It's a ruddy relief. He gave me nothing to work with before I left.'

'So, are you…like-?'

'Lovers? Absolutely.'

Heather chuckled. 'Any good?'

Hannah grinned. 'Sensational. Wish me luck.'

As Hannah left the house and raced downhill to the pub, her mind whizzed and her stomach churned. She halted before the double fronted *Arms* with its honey coloured stone and colourful hanging baskets filled with trailing petunias.

She hesitated to meet Will face to face inside. It was so public in the cosy interior. The locals would recognise her and overhear every word they said. How could they ever talk in private? Praying he might just be on the same wave length and in the outside garden, Hannah stepped around the side of the building. She caught her breath and her whole body collapsed in relief. Prayers really were answered, then.

It was only days but the sight of Will sitting at one of the tables nursing a beer by turns sent her plunging into a shy awkwardness yet filled her with such complete happiness. The afternoon sun shone on his sandy hair bleaching it lighter. He wore a black tee shirt over cargos and appeared completely relaxed.

When he caught sight of her, he didn't say a thing. Just rose from his seat as a slow smile spread across his handsome face and he walked determinedly toward her. Enveloped in his arms, feeling his strength and warmth surround her, Hannah sighed with contentment.

'Hey gorgeous.'

She laughed, flung her arms about his neck and kissed him. 'I won't ask why you're here because I know it's to see me,' she grinned stupidly.

Will took her hand, led her over to his table and drew her down beside him. 'I want to drag you off into the sunset,' he growled, 'and do luscious things to you but I think you need to know Victoria's okay first, am I right?'

Hannah nodded, blown away by Will's thoughtfulness. 'According to Chelsea, she's probably in Monte Carlo.'

'French Riviera. Glitzy.'

'We hope she's fine but we need to check. Heather and I are going later today.'

'How about she stays with her family and I go with you?'

'Really? You'd do that?'

'Of course.'

They enjoyed each other's company alone a while longer, lingering over a cold beer in the midday sunshine, Hannah grateful that Will had arrived to share her burden. Then they walked back uphill to the cottage.

This time, Will officially met Hannah's sisters who sighed over her *chap*, giving a secret thumbs up of approval. Over mugs of tea and biscuits, they discussed plans.

'The flight will only be two hours and, since the glitterati emerge after dark to party and hit the casino, we may even find Victoria tonight.'

'But how do we know where she is? Where do we start?' Hannah frowned.

'Been thinking about that and I may be able to help there. A surfing mate of mine, Richie Hamilton, Emma's brother,' he said to Hannah, 'knows a policeman in London. Before he joined the force and Richie studied medicine, they backpacked all over Europe and Asia together. I'll call him, get a number and see what he can do. No promises but at this point we should try anything. What is Victoria's boyfriend's name, anyone know?'

They all turned to Chelsea.

'Bollocks.' She thought a moment and snapped her fingers. 'Big Greek tycoon, not young but handsome, smooth. Powerful.' Chelsea trailed off. 'Yani something? Um…starts with D, I think.'

'Okay, Yani D. We'll start from there,' Will said. 'And they're on a yacht?'

Chelsea nodded.

Will disappeared into the garden. As they watched him talking on his mobile, Chelsea gasped, 'He is seriously hot.'

'Isn't he just?' Hannah beamed. 'And I went all the way to Australia to find him. Boy was it worth it!'

Will was outside for at least ten minutes but when he returned, he accepted the women's stares with his usual cool poise.

'Right.' He sat on the sofa beside Hannah and explained. 'Phoned Richie back home and got Tom's private number. The cop. Gave him a call, discussed the whole situation. Not desperate as far as we know but we need reassurance. Said he'd phone the Monaco police and see if he could pull in a favour. With the name and nationality and description, he'll try for identifying the guy first and that might hopefully lead to the name of his yacht. The rich and famous are well known and highly visible on the French Riviera and the Med, especially in summer.'

Feeling happier after Will's efforts, Hannah tapped her iPad and searched flights to Nice. 'We'll hire a car from there. I'll drive,' she quipped.

Then it was a scramble. Hannah packed a small overnight bag with summery clothes. Will, not unusually, was already travelling light she noticed with only a bulging carryall. Saying a flurry of goodbyes, they left Chelsea at home, Heather drove them into Oxford for a bus to Heathrow where they made their late afternoon flight to Nice.

On landing on the French Riviera, at the car hire desk, Hannah asked for something sporty. Will eyed her with amusement.

'It's Monte Carlo. We need to blend in and look the part.'

'You're just showing off,' Will chuckled, grinning, as they were handed the keys to a sexy little cabriolet that he itched to drive the moment he saw it.

But a flirty Hannah – who was this woman beside him? – led the way to the vehicle, tossed her bag into the back and jumped in behind the wheel. Looking cheeky and more alive than he had ever seen her, Hannah pushed on huge sunglasses and shook back her hair.

'You navigate.'

'I don't know you,' Will drawled, shaking his head, appreciating the view from the passenger seat.

'Not sure I know myself but I'm getting acquainted,' she laughed.

'Head for Le Port and we'll follow the coast.'

Driving on the right hand side, even for the twelve winding miles following the sea, gave them stunning views of the clear azure Mediterranean waters and the magnificent gleaming white super yachts that graced them.

Because the marina was their most logical destination and best choice for locating Victoria, they headed directly for the Monte Carlo port, anchored with rows of private pleasure boats. Many were sleek and luxurious, with mysterious dark windows in the largest. An ocean liner lay at anchor at the end of the harbour pier further out.

They parked to alight and stretch their legs by the waterfront. Will phoned his police contact, Tom, for any possible news to help their search.

He scribbled something down as he spoken, then hung up. '*Perle de Mer.*'

'Pardon?'

'Yani's yacht. *Sea Pearl.*'

'You've found it!'

'Only the name. It's in the marina. Could be anywhere. We should grab a bite to eat then start walking. Lots of quays out there to explore.'

They bought fish and chips from a brasserie and set off eating them from the paper cone. Later, feet tired from walking, Hannah removed her strappy heeled shoes and let them dangle from her fingers. The soft warm evening air drifted up from the water and the whole port was ablaze now with golden lights as dusk turned to night.

'We might find the yacht but no one on board,' she sighed.

'Then we'll wait,' Will replied with firm optimism.

Not ten minutes later, Hannah let out an 'Oh my God,' and dashed ahead of Will, staring at the name on the side of a double deck yacht with sleek lines, backed up to an outer quay, a short gang plank leading to its lower deck.

'What do we do now?' Hannah whispered.

Will shrugged. 'Get someone's attention. Cabin lights are on down below. Ahoy there,' he called out.

Hannah began to feel terrified and nervous at what they might find. Or not find at all. Suddenly Will stepped brashly aboard and, not wanting to be left behind, Hannah followed.

'Aren't we trespassing?' she squeaked, glancing around at the plush furnishings and gleaming timber deck.

Victoria lived like this? Hannah found it hard to equate her tall classy sister lowering herself to be some old chap's mistress merely to indulge in this luxury. Yes, all quite glamorous but what kind of trade off was that?

Now she discovered she was here and so close to possibly finding her sister, she forgot her cynicism and felt only concern for her safety.

'Victoria?' she called out, drawing confidence from Will's front, standing on deck, hands sunk into his cargo pockets as though he came aboard private yachts all the time. 'Darling, it's Hannah,' she assumed a posh tone, putting on a class she didn't feel but deciding to play a role, see where it led and get this situation sorted.

Suddenly, a burly man appeared at the balcony railing above.

'Oh, hi sweetie.' Hannah tossed back her hair

and beamed. 'Please tell me Victoria is here,' she pouted. 'We've come to party and we'll be crushed if she's out.'

When the big scowling man above, clearly some kind of guard, opened his mouth to speak, Hannah raised a hand and half turned away. 'Please don't tell me she's at the casino.'

'No,' he barked. 'Wait there.'

'Oh sweetie, you're a gem. Tell her Hanny's here and we intend to rave *all night*.' She giggled.

The man disappeared.

Deflecting Will's long look of amused disbelief, Hannah hissed, 'Play along,' holding his arm in support as she replaced her shoes, teetering on the deck, running fingers through her long hair to fluff it out and undoing more top buttons on her summery dress, revealing the lace of her bra beneath.

'Whatever you say. Hanny,' he teased, stunned to watch his woman operate and flirt. If it brought results, he figured, why not? And he was here to keep her safe.

Within moments, inner lights flicked on and Victoria strode across a sumptuous sitting area toward them. Hannah gasped at the silky flimsy negligee, totally transparent, stylish hairdo and heavily made up hardly recognisable face of her sister.

She wanted to weep with relief but, instead, continued playing her part, knowing they were watched and heard, as yet unsure of the extent of Victoria's freedom.

'Vicky, darling,' Hannah kissed her on both cheeks, European style, whispering, 'Play along, okay?'

Victoria winked and a shadow of the sister she knew emerged.

'Hanny, my sweet. You're back! What a delicious surprise,' she said loudly with attitude. 'Are you escaping the wretched English weather?' She gave a deep throaty chuckle. 'Hawke,' she snapped at the guard, 'tell Ivan we want drinks all around down here. Champagne.'

Left alone, if only briefly, Hannah hissed, 'Are you okay?'

Victoria hugged her and nodded, putting a finger to her lips. 'More or less.' She spoke in low tones. 'Word to the wise. Sound carries on the water.'

'Are you here against your will?'

'I was but I suspect not much longer. It was glorious to start with. Yani treated me like a goddess. There's nothing he wouldn't do but about a week ago-' she abruptly stopped when a uniformed servant in white brought a tray of bubbly nestled in an ice bucket and three glass flutes.

'Thank you, Ivan.' He backed away and disappeared. When Hawke hovered, Victoria said sharply, 'Shouldn't you be on the bridge?' and he, too, quietly left.

'As I was saying,' Victoria continued, pouring and handing them each a glass, raising hers in a toast before taking a long sip, 'about a week ago, Yani's roving eye was taken by a gushy young thing called Cherry. All front, no class and only old enough to be his granddaughter. I suspect I'm about to be replaced. I knew I was only a temporary distraction when we met. I was warned but it was rather nice to be spoilt, if only for a time,' she smiled wistfully.

Hannah gaped at her sister's jaded attitude. 'We've been all worried sick about you.'

'Sorry.' Victoria laid a hand on her arm. 'Best not to communicate here. Yani knows everything I do, including what's on my phone.'

'Do you want to get away? Tonight? With us?'

Victoria sparkled with new light. 'I'd love to actually. He won't miss me anyway. He and Cherry are at the casino. He's a high roller and will probably be there all night.'

'We have a car.'

Victoria beamed a creamy smile. 'And who is the other half of *we*? You haven't introduced me.'

'Will Bennett.' He extended a hand. 'Thought it best to let you girls talk it out.'

'You have an accent. How did you two meet?'

'Australia.'

'An Aussie bloke. How exciting. You're quite gorgeous,' Victoria reclined and sipped her champagne, admiring him. 'You would wow them all here and fit right in anywhere on the Riviera.'

'You're very kind but it's not my scene,' he drawled.

They finished their bubbly, refreshing in the summer night, until Victoria rose.

'Stay here. Give me ten or fifteen and I'll join you.'

'Won't it look suspicious if you leave with a bag?'

Victoria laughed. 'Hanny, darling, Yani bought everything I own. I only wish to take my pride.' She grinned wryly, shaking her head. 'Your timing is impeccable. Walking out saves me the face of being dumped but it would have been interesting to see how much I was worth when he paid me off.'

Within half an hour, all three strolled together back to the port boulevard and their parked hire car.

'All good things must end,' Victoria sighed, clutching a large designer carryall. 'I believe I'm finally over all this.' She glanced behind them to the marina, glittering yachts and laughter of the hedonistic wealthy. 'Time to go home.'

'The girls are waiting for news of you. Here, use my phone and call them,' Hannah said.

As she handed it over and Victoria strolled away to chat to her sisters, Will asked, 'So, where would my future wife like to go next?'

Hannah raised her eyebrows and bubbled

with delight. 'Are you sure?'

'You're the woman of my heart and I love you deeply. I'm never letting you go again.'

They sealed the arrangement on the sidewalk, oblivious to the noise of surrounding people, diners and a continuous stream of classy traffic with a hungrily passionate kiss.

Afterwards, Hannah said, 'As if you didn't know, the answer is *Yes* and…um…somewhere exotic.'

'You mean like, say, Morocco exotic?'

Hannah smiled. 'Sounds perfect but my sisters will kill me if they're not bridesmaids.'

'Then let's have the honeymoon first and the wedding later.'

'Done.'

At that moment, Victoria returned.

'Victoria.' Hannah jingled the cabriolet keys in front of her. 'Here are your wheels back to Nice to fly home.'

Her sister didn't look particularly surprised. 'What shall I tell the girls?'

'That Will and I are engaged and we'll be cruising the Mediterranean.'

'Winging it,' Will added, sliding an arm around his fiancé's waist.

'Bloody wonderful news, Hannah. You're way overdue for a life of your own.'

Why had Hannah not known and seen this herself much sooner? 'Thanks,' she whispered, as they hugged goodbye. 'Tell the others we'll be home. Eventually.'

Will and Hannah grabbed their bags from the back seat of the car, then Victoria climbed in and sped away.

'Where to now?' Hannah asked. My goodness, once she would have needed to know. Now she couldn't care less.

'Lovely waterfront hotels over there. Let's take a punt, shall we?'

As they strolled, arms around each other, Will said, 'Emma and Mal will expect me back for their wedding in spring.'

'But not that I'll be with you,' she grinned. 'We have lots of lovely weeks to fill in until then.'

'What about your job?'

'Oh, I chucked that in. I'm officially unemployed but I have my super and a little nest egg after the cottage sells. I'll get by,' she glanced up at him, 'and I've met this man…'

'Well then, if you're not doing anything particular in your life in the immediate future,' Will growled, 'we could consider starting a family. That would keep us both occupied.'

'Food for thought,' Hannah agreed softly, thrilling inside, stopping mid stride to demand a kiss from the man she loved.

A dreamy honeymoon.

A romantic wedding, wherever.

Children. She sighed.

Hannah's holiday had been a right success and the future glowed bright with promise.